PORTRAIT *of* *a* HUSBAND *with the* ASHES *of his* WIFE

ESSENTIAL TRANSLATIONS SERIES 42 

Canada Council for the Arts | Conseil des Arts du Canada

ONTARIO ARTS COUNCIL
CONSEIL DES ARTS DE L'ONTARIO
an Ontario government agency
un organisme du gouvernement de l'Ontario

Canada

Guernica Editions Inc. acknowledges the support
of the Canada Council for the Arts and the Ontario Arts Council.
The Ontario Arts Council is an agency of the Government of Ontario.
We acknowledge the financial support of the Government of Canada
through the National Translation Program for Book Publishing, an initiative
of the Roadmap for Canada's Official Languages 2013-2018:
Education, Immigration, Communities, for our translation activities.
We acknowledge the financial support of the Government of Canada.
Nous reconnaissons l'appui financier du gouvernement du Canada.

PORTRAIT *of* *a* HUSBAND *with the* ASHES *of his* WIFE

Pan Bouyoucas

Translated from the French by

Sheila Fischman

TORONTO • BUFFALO • LANCASTER (U.K.)
2018

Original title: *Portrait d'un mari avec les cendres de sa femme* (2010)

Michael Mirolla, editor
Allen Jomoc, Jr., cover design
David Moratto, interior design
Guernica Editions Inc.
1569 Heritage Way, Oakville, (ON), Canada L6M 2Z7
2250 Military Road, Tonawanda, N.Y. 14150-6000 U.S.A.
www.guernicaeditions.com

Distributors:
University of Toronto Press Distribution,
5201 Dufferin Street, Toronto (ON), Canada M3H 5T8
Gazelle Book Services, White Cross Mills
High Town, Lancaster LA1 4XS U.K.

First edition.
Printed in Canada.

Legal Deposit—Third Quarter
Library of Congress Catalog Card Number: 2018932960
Library and Archives Canada Cataloguing in Publication
Bouyoucas, Pan
[Portrait d'un mari avec les cendres de sa femme. English]
Portrait of a husband with the ashes of his wife / Pan Bouyoucas ; translated by Sheila Fischman. -- First edition.

(Essential translations series ; 42)
Translation of: Portrait d'un mari avec les cendres de sa femme.
Issued in print and electronic formats.
ISBN 978-1-77183-263-2 (softcover).--ISBN 978-1-77183-264-9 (EPUB). --
ISBN 978-1-77183-265-6 (Kindle)

I. Fischman, Sheila, translator II. Title. III. Title: Portrait d'un mari avec les cendres de sa femme. English. IV. Series: Essential translations series ; 42

PS8553.O89P6713 2018 C843'.54 C2018-900824-5 C2018-900825-3

1

ALMA JONCAS WAS one of the most acclaimed, the most venerated actresses in all Quebec. Until the day she turned fifty.

A tough moment for any actress whose life marks time with her roles.

A tough moment too for her spouse who must constantly feed her self-esteem and her hopes so that she won't collapse into depression.

Doctor Alexandre Maras, ophthalmological surgeon, mentioned the name of his wife to all the producers and directors among his patients. All replied that Alma was a great artist, that they would definitely call her when a suitable role came along. But Alma's telephone was silent and all signs suggested that her age—too mature for a young lover, not old enough for a granny—would confine her to the worst fate that can be inflicted on an actress: invisibility.

Alma was driven to despair but refused to resign herself. Rather than let time mould her for the granny and old nurse parts, she decided to hurry things up by stuffing herself with everything that would make her put on weight.

Instead of filling out though, Alma began to lose the little bit of fat she had on her body.

She told her husband:

"I want you to put my ashes in the place where I was happiest."

Doctor Maras scorned the resignation that actors are partial to when they're not working and recommended that she see her doctor. But Alma was convinced that the stage was her sole salvation, that she just needed a good, meaty part and she would get her strength back.

Finally, the phone rang: Pauline Brunet, artistic director of the Théâtre Orphée and a friend of Alma, offering her the title role in *The House of Bernarda Alba*.

It was a role as beautiful as it was rare for an actress of her age, but exhausting too, and Doctor Maras feared for his wife's health.

Alma replied that what was most exhausting in her line of work was not working.

And in fact as soon as she started rehearsals her eyes gleamed, her back straightened, her voice sparkled, and the butterfly that age was getting ready to turn into a caterpillar flew again.

On the night of the premiere, despite a severe bout of stage fright and stomach cramps, Alma played García Lorca's tyrannical matriarch with such self-assurance that the next day, the critics couldn't stop praising her performance, describing it as the most luminous moment of the theatrical season.

It was April 24, spring had finally arrived, the show was an overwhelming success, and every night when the curtain fell, applause and bravos called the star back onstage at least five times.

Alma was feeling a numbness in her extremities but could not for a moment imagine the heavy cost that her success would impose and didn't speak to her doctor until the day after the last performance.

Her family doctor sent her to a cardiologist, who diagnosed a contraction of the aortic valve so far advanced that blood could barely flow between the left ventricle and the aorta.

In other words:

"You should have had an operation three months ago."

Back home, Alma prepared a candlelit dinner and put on a yellow silk dress with a décolletage that was an enchantment, as much to please herself as to arouse her husband, because soon her torso would be butchered and never again would she be able to wear a plunging neckline.

Two glasses of wine later, intoxicated more by anxiety than by alcohol and the fragrant breath of lilac with which spring had filled her garden, she said to her husband:

"My love, make me fly. Even if the operation is successful, for a long time I'll be nothing but a sea gull with broken wings."

Her eyes were glowing but her shortness of breath and Doctor Maras's expertise advised him not to comply.

But he also knew that when his wife got something in her head she would pursue it until she was satisfied. He concentrated then on the pleasure he could give her without her having to exhaust herself.

Alma murmured, Yes, yes. Then, her face transformed by orgasm, she stiffened in her husband's arms.

Doctor Maras called 9-1-1, then did all he could to bring her back to life.

In vain.

2

AFTER THE PARAMEDICS had taken the body away, Doctor Maras called on her cell phone Mélissa, their only child, who had gone out that night with her boyfriend. He told her:

"I killed her."

"What are you talking about?"

"She wanted to make love ..."

"That's so sweet. She wanted to make love one last time."

"But it killed her. I killed her."

"No, papa, no, you helped her to die happy."

The candles Alma had lit were still burning in the dining room which barely an hour ago was filled with life. Doctor Maras didn't have the heart to blow them out or to watch them burn up either and he went out into the garden to wait for their daughter to show up.

Alma's garden ...

During these past three years of waiting and worry, one bud was enough to make her forget every jobless winter she'd just endured. But gardening for her wasn't a hobby indulged in when nothing was happening in her career to take her mind off her boredom. It was a passion to which she devoted herself as much as to her roles, fiercely and with extraordinary excitement, and even when she was working she spent her free hours raking, sowing, watering, weeding, pruning and staking.

"It's pure creation," she said of gardening. "True magic."

The previous year her garden had won first prize in the *Montreal in Bloom* competition "for the impressive diversity of annuals and the synergy of climbing plants whose shapes and colours make a dynamic garden as a whole."

This year she had opted for a diversity of vegetables and perennials which in her opinion would create an atmosphere full of gaiety that would win her her second first prize.

Next year, for their 25th wedding anniversary, she intended to plant two plum trees.

Doctor Maras recollected all that and when his daughter arrived he told her:

"She asked me to put her ashes in the place where she was the happiest so I'm going to bury them here, in her garden. She will stay with us for the winter and she'll waken in the spring."

Mélissa hugged her father and both of them finally allowed the tears they were holding back to flow.

3

THE FUNERAL WAS held six days later, at the church of Notre-Dame-du-Bon-Conseil where it seemed everyone who had worked with Alma over the past thirty years had come together to pay her a final tribute. Also present were the mayor of Montreal, the mayoress of her district, Quebec's Minister of Cultural Affairs, some colleagues of Doctor Maras, some friends of Mélissa too, and of course Alma's close family members: her unmarried sister, Carmen, a notary in La Malbaie where the three Joncas children had been born; her brother Zak, a sculptor who lived in the Montreal suburb of Saint-Hilaire, accompanied by his young wife Liza and Ezekiel, their six-year-old son; and two female cousins with their spouses. There was no one from the family of Doctor Maras because he had only one sister, Hélène, and she lived in Paris where she was responsible for academic and cultural relations at the Canadian embassy.

A homily was delivered by the officiant, followed by tributes. The first was from Zak. He had never seen Alma act in the theatre, only on television, yet he called her a great tragedian, because, he said, even as a child her back was always erect when she cried.

"Today though she is singing. Do you hear her?" he asked, pricking his ear towards the huge maple trees that surrounded the church, their dense foliage full of birds. "That chirping is Alma telling us she loves us and asking those who love her not to hold her back with sad thoughts because it is with an infinite joy that she is continuing on the road that leads to the Creator."

Carmen, who wasn't very fond of her brother, whispered into the ear of Doctor Maras:

"So the hypocrite speaks with the dead now, does he?"

Carmen would have liked her brother-in-law to speak in the name of the family, but all Doctor Maras would have said in public could be summed up in one sentence: She was my sun. Before that even crossed his mind he was rejecting it, because he still had another sun, his daughter, and he wasn't going to go into lengthy explanations, he who was never long-winded and had always expressed his love better with actions than with words. And so he let the others celebrate Alma. It was perhaps the last time they would think about her whereas he would have her in his thoughts every day.

After Zak, Pauline Brunet, artistic director of the Théâtre Orphée, spoke about her friendship with the dead woman since their student days at the National Theatre School, then about Alma's contribution to Quebec theatre. She also mentioned some of her accomplishments and concluded by uttering the line that every night made the audience shiver when Alma proclaimed it with her deep voice before the curtain fell on *The House of Bernarda Alba*:

> *And no tears. Death must be stared at straight in the face. Silence! Do you hear? Silence, silence, I say! Silence!*

Those words took Doctor Maras right back to the moment when he had heard them for the first time, in their house. When she was memorizing a text Alma would sometimes repeat the lines while going about other business. Sometimes too she would ask her husband to give her her cues. At first he stammered, but with time he had gained confidence, sometimes letting himself get carried away by emotion, especially when there were rhymes.

> *No, you detest me now; and your deep art*
> *Fears to owe a thing to my fond heart.*

He had spoken those words by Racine with such ferocity that Alma had laughed so hard he could see her tonsils.

Today, while actors and actresses were singing Alma's praises, one with an anecdote, another reading lines from one of the characters she had played, Doctor Maras, thinking back to the past, told himself: "Never again will I give her cues, never again will I hear her wonderful laughter in the house."

4

AT THE RECEPTION following the religious service, when Zak learned what Doctor Maras intended to do with Alma's ashes, he told him:

"You're right to want to leave them in a garden. My sister adored gardens and the mere scent of freshly-mown grass would make her heart race. But the garden that Alma liked best is the one you had in Saint-Hilaire. Her Montreal garden was more a consolation than a pleasure because these last years both her work and her health experienced only lows."

The house in Saint-Hilaire was the first one Alma and her husband had lived in. Subsequently they had sold it to Zak because Doctor Maras, who had grown up in a densely populated part of Montreal, couldn't get used to the suburbs. Which was why Zak went on to say:

"On the other hand, when you were living in Saint-Hilaire, her career was at its peak, she was young and so much in love that she held your hand even when you were on your bikes. It was there too that she became a mother and in that garden that she saw her child take her first steps. The house isn't yours any more but it doesn't belong to strangers. It belongs to her brother. I will put in a beautiful corner for her in the garden, and you and Mélissa will be able to come and visit her as often as you want and observe the changing seasons with her, as she loved to do when she was alive."

Hearing that, Carmen told her brother:

"Alma chose to live in Saint-Hilaire because the open spaces, the orchards, and the wooded hills all reminded her of the countryside at La Malbaie where she'd spent the most wonderful moments of her life when she was a child."

"You've got a hell of a nerve," Zak said, "to claim today of all days that Alma wasn't happy with her husband and their child."

"That's not what I said," Carmen replied. "Anyway, if Alma was happiest with Alexandre and Mélissa, why do you want her ashes at your place?"

"I just explained why!" her brother said.

Those two couldn't abide each other at all and they were about to resume their name-calling when Pauline Brunet interrupted:

"You two obviously didn't know your sister very well or you'd realize that she was happiest when she was working. That was where she found meaning and justification for her life: on a stage, in her dressing room, in the wings, backstage. It was that environment with its smells, its commotion, its lights that brought her the greatest satisfaction. So much so that she gambled her health on Bernarda Alba rather than stay at home observing the changing seasons, watering plants and talking to them.

Listening to you one would think you never saw her on stage. You probably never did, or you'd have known that Alma never wept, neither with her back erect nor bent double nor lying down. Alma wasn't one of those pathetic actresses who make up their eyes with glycerine as if talent were measured by the quantity of tears an actor can shed."

"I live too far from Montreal to come to evening performances," Zak said.

"I don't like dramas and tragedies," Carmen said. "But I've seen all the comedies Alma performed in, in Quebec City, Chicoutimi, and La Malbaie. And the theatre in La Malbaie is a stone's throw from her childhood garden."

"What?!" Pauline Brunet said, with the contempt of the director of a repertory theatre for light comedy. "You want to scatter the ashes of a great actress like her in a summer theatre?"

"Certainly," Carmen replied. "And I have proof that it's what my sister would have wanted."

Then she left, promising her brother-in-law that she would send him the next day, special delivery, irrefutable evidence that Alma would have wanted her ashes buried at La Malbaie.

Zak left the reception two minutes later, saying he was going to draw the monument that he would erect in his garden to receive the ashes of his favourite sister.

Pauline Brunet also hastened to leave, to convene the board of the Orphée and discuss with its members the best way that her theatre could honour the ashes of Alma Joncas.

5

DOCTOR MARAS WAS a man who once he had taken on a task also took on all its demands, all its repercussions. But the task had to be clear, for he loathed anything vague, anything confused. And so he spent the rest of the day and a considerable part of the night turning the pages of the past in search of a word, a phrase, or an anecdote that would have dispelled the doubt that Zak, Carmen, and Pauline Brunet had sowed in his mind. Conscientious and meticulous, he read the reviews in the press devoted to his wife and listened to recordings of interviews she'd given on radio and television.

He was searching for a clue, a lead. There were dozens in Alma's declarations that brought him more blurriness than they dispelled.

"Alma Joncas is the very image of perfect happiness," evoked her joy at acting in Paris where, as a young actress, she'd had a run of four months at the Théâtre national de Chaillot.

"Alma's Bliss" talked about her affection for Mélissa, who was still a baby, and for her husband.

"Drunk on Happiness" a few months later recounted her nomination in Cannes for the award for best actress in a leading role, in a film by Serge Groslin.

Indeed, rare were the articles and interviews in which the word happiness did not appear at least once, whether it was about gardening, her childhood in La Malbaie, or her trips abroad. Even about the new kitchen she'd had put in. As if this woman, passionate by nature, loved everything she did because she only embarked upon that which excited her and added life to her life.

Bewildered and weary, Doctor Maras went out into the garden to freshen his thoughts.

Spring, heedless of the grief and torments of man, was scenting the air with lilacs.

In the sky sailed by a solitary cloud.

And for a moment the poor man thought he saw in it the face of his beloved.

She was looking at him reproachfully, as if to say: "I am the woman with whom for twenty-four years you shared the table, the bed, and the intimacy and you don't know where I was happiest?"

6

THE NEXT MORNING, Doctor Maras announced to his daughter that he had made up his mind: He would bury the ashes in their garden.

"If Alma didn't specify the place where she was happiest," he said, "it's because she trusted my judgment, for after twenty-four years of married life I knew her better than anyone else."

But no sooner had he drunk his coffee than the phone began to ring and rang without let-up all morning. All the actresses in *The House of Bernarda Alba* called to tell him, each in turn, that Alma had been happiest when she was acting, more particularly at the Orphée. Some even swore that they'd heard her say, "as if she sensed that the end was approaching," that actors' ashes should always be left at their favourite theatre.

Doctor Maras also had a call from Raymond Cholette, a producer at Radio-Canada and, like Alma, a native of the Charlevoix region who agreed with Zak's declaration.

"Show business is a small world," he said, "rumours get around quickly, and when I got wind of the argument that broke out after the funeral yesterday, I felt that I had a duty to call you. Of course I'd have liked to see Alma buried at La Malbaie. But I have to confess that, when she called me a few months ago looking for work, she confided that she'd spent the most wonderful moments of her life in Saint-Hilaire."

No one called in favour of La Malbaie and, when the bell rang just before noon, Doctor Maras thought it was the mail carrier come to deliver the conclusive proof that Carmen had promised to send him.

But when he opened the door he saw a sixty-something woman with hennaed hair and bracelets all up her arms.

"I've come to offer my condolences," she said. "Alma and I saw a lot of each other in the past year."

She gave him her card.

"If you ever need my services, don't hesitate to come and see me. I live two blocks away."

Doctor Maras looked at the card and frowned when he read: Madame Élias. Clairvoyant. Medium.

Many actresses ask for your Zodiac sign before they ask what type of work you do. Alma was an exception. Or so thought Doctor Maras, who believed he knew Alma better than anyone. He was less certain after Madame Élias had left, when he asked Mélissa if she knew that her mother consulted a clairvoyant.

"Yes, I knew," his daughter replied. "Mama was depressed at not working and she wanted to find out about the future. She never mentioned those consultations because she knew you'd have laughed."

Doctor Maras wondered if there were other things that his wife hadn't told him and he called Aline Diamond, Alma's agent and friend, to ask her.

Aline Diamond replied:

"You are all right to think that Alma was happiest in the places you've just mentioned. Over the years, depending on her mood, she recalled every one of them as being the site of perfect happiness. In my opinion, the best solution would be to scatter a handful of ashes in Saint-Hilaire, a handful at the Orphée, a handful at La Malbaie—and the rest in your garden."

As a physician and surgeon, Doctor Maras was well aware of what the ashes of a human being amount to: barely two kilos of the calcareous part of the bones crushed and sifted, the rest transformed into gas and dust particles that fly away into the flames. Still he winced at the thought of scattering those two kilos of his beloved's calcium to the four corners of the province.

"I'm going to put all the ashes in one place," he told his daughter. "But the place that my heart and my mind steer me to isn't necessarily the one that Alma would have picked. So I'm going to revisit each of the other three places before I make my decision."

Without the slightest suspicion that with those words he would set off a chain of events that would change forever the course of his life and his daughter's.

IT WAS ON the stage of the Orphée that he had seen Alma for the first time. She was playing Martha in *Le Malentendu* by Camus. The brother of the play's director, a friend of Doctor Maras, had invited him to the première. The doctor didn't know a thing about theatre and thought that the talent of an actress was determined by how well she could figure out what to do with the words that were lent to her so that for two hours the audience thought that she was someone else. But Alma had been so tragic and noble as a dejected girl without love that in her mouth every word became rich and sacred, every gesture took on a meaning that dignified it, and he was still profoundly overwhelmed by her performance when his friend took him backstage to introduce him to his brother, the director, and the actors.

Today the Orphée box office was closed, the lobby deserted. The theatre too. Save for a woman's voice coming to him from the back of the corridor leading to the office of Pauline Brunet. A bad-tempered voice saying:

"So the diva wants her ashes left where she was the happiest. How touching! How romantic! How annoying! Yes, annoying! Because the only times I saw Alma Joncas happy were when she was pissing off everybody. And with her last wishes she's still pissing us off from the other side of death."

The voice was that of Nicole Gouin, a playwright in her forties whom Montreal's entire theatre world had been praising to the skies ever since she'd enjoyed a certain success in Paris. Except Alma. Though she'd have given anything to go back on stage she had refused to act in a play by Nicole Gouin because she thought it was nothing but a sea of beautiful sentences every one of which claimed to hold a profound truth.

"I can't take any more of those fancy, hollow lines where every snore is assumed to be an illumination," she had told the dramatist. "I want a story, characters, conflict, not that mush about your every turd and fart."

Alma wasn't one to mince words and she was never reluctant to give free rein to her opinions. Which slams a lot of doors in the diffident small world of the theatre. But actress though she was, capable of every ruse and audacity on stage, off-stage she couldn't lie and play-act to save her life. Once she had brought a tin of foie gras home from Paris. When the customs officer asked if she had any meat, she had turned bright red and was searched to the very linings of her suitcase and her coat.

Alma was just as incapable of pretending, or of holding her tongue at least, when for instance she was asked what she thought of a show. And when her husband criticized her once for having offended the artistic director of a theatre with her remarks, she had replied:

"Are courage and integrity the monopoly of the characters we play?"

"I'm not asking you to lie or to betray your convictions. You couldn't do it and that makes me very happy. But sometimes it's wiser to be right silently even if it's just to avoid offending the convictions of others."

Alma tried silence.

A week later, she told her husband:

"I know you have to be something of a whore in this job but silence only fosters mediocrity. If a show is rotten, it's rotten, and if I'm asked what I think I won't say the contrary to keep my name on the guest list."

That's how she was made, Alma. An open book. And now Nicole Gouin was getting her own back.

"A theatre's not a graveyard or a museum," she shrieked at the end of the corridor. "But Alma Joncas never understood that. Which was why she defended her classics so fervently, with all their fake conflicts, their fake actions and subterfuges, when the duty of theatre today is to force spectators to plunge into the depths of their own subconscious to find their genuine self in the silence of silence."

"This theatre is also a business," Pauline Brunet told her. "A business that has been piling up debts ever since the budget cuts by the Culture Ministry and I doubt that during this recession we can absorb those debts by plunging into the depths of our subconscious. On the other hand, Alma's ashes can double the number of subscribers. Quadruple them even if other actors announce that they'll leave their funeral urns to us."

"And where will you place your dear Alma's urn? On stage, I suppose, and the audience will observe a minute's silence before every performance. Or maybe you'll keep it under your desk so you'll always have her between your legs."

"Don't be vulgar, jewel. You're talking about a dead woman who was also a good friend."

"If you loved her that much, why not use her ashes to stuff your tits? She would always be next to your heart and I'd stop feeling as if I'm kissing prunes."

"Stop, my love, you're killing me."

"Yuck! Just thinking about it turns my stomach. Your old prunes, the cracks in your skin, your oozing lips, your mouse squeaks—I feel as if I'm in a sarcophagus when I lie in our bed. For consolation, I had our theatre. Now you want to turn it into a mausoleum too. But I won't let myself be buried in it!"

The office door opened wide.

And it was Pauline Brunet's turn to shriek.

"I'll do whatever you want! Come back, Nicole! I'll do whatever you want!"

8

IN THE TIME it took to go home, Doctor Maras had erased Pauline Brunet and her theatre from his mind.

Mélissa was sitting at Alma's dressing table. Shoulders hunched, eyes red and swollen, she was holding a brush that still contained the hairs her mother had left there the last time she'd used it.

"I miss her so much ..."

He stroked her head and promised himself to decide quickly about the ashes so that he could look after his child who had also been hit hard by the tragedy.

"Still no word from Carmen?"

"No. But Zak called. He worked on Mama's monument all last night and all day today and he invited us to Saint-Hilaire tomorrow to look at his sketches."

As he had not received from Carmen irrefutable proof that Alma had been happiest in the place of her childhood, he wouldn't have to go to La Malbaie. If he hadn't received the call from Raymond Cholette yesterday, he'd have forgotten Saint-Hilaire as well and buried the ashes in the garden that night. He knew though that, if he didn't see their first house again, the call from Raymond Cholette would always gnaw at him.

"What would you like for supper tonight?"

"I'm not hungry."

Nor was he, all he wanted was to have something else to think about, to take everything out of the realm of emotion and back to the everyday so that it would feel as if life were continuing.

But his daughter chose to go to bed.

Twelve hours later, Mélissa was still shut away in her room and refusing to go with him to Saint-Hilaire.

"You haven't set foot in that house since we moved to Montreal," he told her. "You should see it again one last time. For Mama."

He loathed that kind of argument, playing on emotions, but he didn't have the heart to leave her there, moping in her bed. To mollify her he reminded her of all the love that her mother had invested in their house in Saint-Hilaire, all the sleepless nights spent rocking her baby, all the hours she'd devoted to playing in the garden with her little tot. He even told her what he'd heard at the Orphée the night before and for the first time since Alma's death, they both laughed.

An hour later, Doctor Maras was not laughing at all.

On both sides of the highway to Saint-Hilaire apple trees in blossom covered the ground as far as the eye could see. The air was perfumed, and dazzling light filled the sky from horizon to horizon. Just like the day when Alma had brought him to see the house that she wanted to live in. She became impassioned at the thought of moving to Saint-Hilaire, as if she intended to redecorate the entire region. She talked and quivered so much behind the wheel that it was not the landscape but his life that Doctor Maras saw passing before his eyes.

"Zak was probably right," he finally admitted. "In every image of your mother that I have from then she was brimming over with enthusiasm and joy, with energy and a sense of purpose."

Mélissa squeezed his hand. It was her turn to raise her father's morale.

"Wait and see the garden," she told him. "Everything depends on the state it's in."

9

ALMA AND ALEXANDRE'S first house ...

The front was still the same, the street too. Deserted, as it had been long ago. Never had he got used to it. Yes, in Saint-Hilaire the gardens were bigger and more fragrant, the birds chirped all day long and at night the sky was starrier, but he needed to hear human voices, to see people, and not just behind the wheel but here they never went on foot. Didn't even need to walk the dog. It was more oppressive during the long winter months when the snow muffled the few human sounds that came to him in summer. Besides that, he had to go to bed and get up an hour earlier to arrive at the hospital where he operated every morning, while in the evening no sooner would he arrive home than already it was time to put his child to bed.

Zak and Liza greeted them with open arms. As did their guests. There were around twenty, including Raymond Cholette, the Radio-Canada producer to whom Alma had confided that she'd spent the most wonderful moments of her life in Saint-Hilaire. There was also someone with the look of an apostle, whom Zak introduced as Frère Isaïe, spiritual leader of the Alliance universelle pour la Vie, a movement based on justice and peace, wherein members would come together around a global union wherein all creatures would be esteemed and loved for what they were.

"That's all very well," Doctor Maras said to his brother-in-law, "but why is he here? Why are all of them here?"

"Why, for Alma," Zak replied. "And for you and Mélissa. They love you."

"I hope they don't start hugging and kissing me," Doctor Maras said to his daughter.

"You're the one who insisted on coming, so be quiet," she responded.

A table had been set with salads, fruit, and pastries because, like his biblical namesake, Frère Isaïe dreamed of the lion eating straw with the ox and insisted that all the members of his Alliance be vegetarians like him. But before they tackled the buffet, Zak invited everyone to come to his studio to look at sketches of the monument he suggested putting up in memory of his sister.

"I've never worked so fast or got such good results in such a short time," he told them. "It's as if Alma were guiding my eye and my hand."

Everyone was impressed. Even Mélissa who, seeing her uncle in a new light, told him:

"I envy artists like you and my mother. Your path is already laid out by your talent."

"You too, young lady, you will do great things," Frère Isaïe said, clasping her shoulders. "I see your aura. An aura as dazzling as the ones with which we adorn the saints on icons."

Liza was listening with a beatific expression as if golden eggs were emerging from the mouth of her spiritual father.

"Frère Isaïe has the gift," she murmured to Doctor Maras. "I'd always suspected that I came from another world. Frère Isaïe has confirmed it."

Meanwhile, Frère Isaïe was saying to Mélissa:

"There are two kinds of individual: those who think that they could walk on water if they put their minds to it and those who have to be constantly reminded that they have two feet. That's all you need to understand, my child, and the talent the Creator has given you, that gift which is hidden in you, will blossom just as mine has done, late in the day as well, after I had a vision."

Mélissa, who adored that kind of story, forgot her sorrow for a moment and asked the man to tell her what had happened to him. And while he was describing the vision that had transformed his life and the others were attacking the buffet, Doctor Maras made his way to the garden.

Had it not been for Mont Saint-Hilaire facing him, he'd have sworn that he had taken the wrong exit.

While everywhere else the trees were in blossom, Alma's once luxuriant garden was now a desert. Literally. The three neighbouring gardens too. It was not only the fences separating them that had been torn out but also the trees and shrubs, to make the four lots into one flat, open field that had been covered with sand. As well, in the very centre had been planted palm trees made of some synthetic material, as if to create an oasis.

In vain Doctor Maras tried to picture Alma as a young actress, a young wife and mother; the only image of her that he could see was the last one he had held onto—Alma at her moment of bliss murmuring: Yes, yes, before she expired.

As a result, the anguish that had gripped him as he approached Saint-Hilaire fell away and when his daughter joined him, he smiled at her again. He also smiled at the guests who were emerging from the house behind his daughter. He smiled at Zak and Liza who had erased every sign of Alma from their property. He even smiled at Frère Isaïe who, addressing Melissa and her father, said:

"My brother, my daughter, I have the pleasure of telling you that the monument in memory of our beloved sister, Alma, whom the Eternal, our Creator, has received in His glory, will be ready to be inaugurated on the evening of the feast of la Saint-Jean, known as well as the time of enchantments."

"Hallelujah!" replied his flock in unison.

"Now, my children, form a circle. And hand in hand, let us pray to our beloved sister Alma and ask her where she would like the monument to her memory to be erected."

He gave one hand to Mélissa and offered the other to her father.

Rather than take it, Doctor Maras said to him:

"Thank you for your welcome and your love, but this is not the place where we will leave her ashes."

A murmur of disappointment rose from beneath the fake palm trees.

"You sure gotta bitching black karma, ain'tcha!" Liza exclaimed, losing briefly her beatific expression and her affected accent.

Frère Isaïe, unaccustomed to being contradicted, glared at the rebel as if to intimidate him into retracting.

Doctor Maras turned his back on him and said to Zak, who was regarding him with clenched jaw:

"I thank you for your invitation and your drawings. But this oasis, welcoming though it is, is no longer my wife's garden."

10

A FEW MINUTES later, en route to Montreal, he said to his daughter:

"Carmen was right to be wary of Zak. Just like Pauline with her theatre, he only wanted the ashes to raise the profile of his sect, and he asked Raymond Cholette to call me and say that Alma had confided to him that she'd spent the most beautiful moments of her life in Saint-Hilaire."

"That'll teach you to listen to others instead of to your own heart," Mélissa replied.

Her father did not defend himself or explain that to hear his heart he would first have to silence the doubts in his head. Instead he erased the visit from his mind. Except for the remark that his daughter had made to Zak: "I envy artists like you and my mother. Your path is already laid out by your talent."

Why had she said that, when she'd just completed her first year of medical school? Surely it wasn't sycophancy: that was not her way. He would talk about it with her later, at the house. When they had buried the ashes in the garden he would have plenty of time to broach the subject.

Unfortunately, a large envelope from Priority Post that appeared in the mailbox stopped him.

The envelope contained two sheets of paper.

The first was a hand-written note that read:

> *Here is the proof I mentioned. See you soon. Carmen.*

The second was a photocopy of an interview Alma had given to the *Journal de Charlevoix*. In it she spoke mainly about the comedy in which she'd acted at the summer theatre in La Malbaie two decades earlier.

> *It was the most wonderful summer of my life. Utter happiness. It was before the casino opened and we were the only attraction in town. Everyone came to see us and every night the other actors and I were invited all over and we ate and drank and danced until three a.m. I lived in my father's house and that summer, I realized why I hadn't stayed in France, where I'd been offered roles in both theatre and film.*

The interview was dated barely a year earlier.

When Doctor Maras showed his daughter the two sheets of paper, she said:

"Here we go again!"

With a lump in his throat, her father replied:

"Don't you think I'd have liked to know that she was happiest with me? 'It was the most wonderful summer of my life.' The most wonderful summer of her life! When she'd always told me that her most wonderful summer had been the one we'd spent in Greece, when you were five."

Mélissa had never seen her father so disconsolate.

"She told me too that she'd spent the most beautiful summer of her life in Greece, papa," she said. "So let's bury the ashes here and that will be that."

That was also his wish, poor soul, but being the kind of man he was, he replied:

"I have to be clear about it in my own mind. Your mother wanted her ashes to be buried in the place where she was the happiest, and I intend to respect her wishes."

Two minutes later he called his sister-in-law to tell her they were coming. But when he hung up, Mélissa told him she wouldn't go to La Malbaie with him and that this time, nothing would make her change her mind.

"You'll come back with the ashes, like we did from Saint-Hilaire because deep down you know that you want to bury them here. Why should I drive for five hours for nothing?"

And so he got back on the road by himself, bringing with him the urn containing the ashes, convinced that he would leave them at La Malbaie, and he drove for five hours without a single glance at the landscapes that he crossed.

Without seeing either that all the evidence of Alma's happiness provided by others was in the process of forging his own unhappiness and that of his child.

11

CARMEN HAD LAID out the plates and cutlery on the garden table, opened a bottle of wine, and ordered in the finest dishes because, unlike her sister, she hated to cook.

"I hope you'll come more often now that the ashes will be here," she told her brother-in-law. "You're the only family I have. Alma is gone. Zak, I can't even look at his photo. And this house belongs to your daughter. As I have no children, I'll put it in her name."

Unlike her first garden as a married woman in Saint-Hilaire, the one at the house where Alma had grown up was unchanged. It was actually more beautiful and four times the size of her garden in Montreal. In addition, the top of the cliffs offered an unbroken view of the harbour at Pointe-au-Pic and the St. Lawrence River that flowed a hundred metres below, immense. The gallery where Alma, as a young girl with eyes full of dreams, had announced to her parents that she wanted to become an actress was still there too, as was the grove behind which she had exchanged her first kiss. The boy, René Poitras, was the son of the woman who did the cleaning at the

Joncas house. He opened a bar and restaurant and, during the summer when she'd acted at La Malbaie, after each performance Alma usually went there to eat and drink and dance.

Doctor Maras had known all that for more than twenty years. Today though he wondered for the first time if that summer had been the most wonderful of Alma's life because it had been the summer of her first love. The first man too who had given her cues when, at age eighteen, she had to memorize two scenes for her audition at the National Theatre School.

"Does René Poitras still have his restaurant?"

"Yes, all the food on this table is from René's."

"Alma must have eaten there often when she came to La Malbaie ..."

"Every night. And when those two got together they could drink and laugh and gossip till breakfast."

Doctor Maras pushed away his plate.

"It was a long drive. I'm too tired to eat."

"Please don't go to bed. I don't often have the chance to eat with someone ..."

The two sisters had little in common, and not just physically. As much as Alma was bubbly, exuberant and full of life, her sister was reserved, withdrawn and subdued. They had the same eyes, though, the same hair, and in other circumstances he would have begged Carmen not to leave the table, so much did her eyes and hair drown him in memories, to the point of imagining Alma in the flesh at his side. But tonight, though it was only nine o'clock and still daylight, he decided to go to bed and rose from the table, saying:

"Eat at René's!"

He had always been able to control his feelings. One of the qualities that Alma admired about him—she who could blow up over the slightest thing and who had an art for making mountains out of molehills. It was clear that all of her husband's qualities hadn't been enough for her to be faithful to him. And as his sister-in-law had been the complicit witness to that infidelity, he couldn't stop himself from saying, viciously:

"Eat at René's!"

Carmen, her voice weary now, replied:

"I no longer find his erotic obsessions funny. Maybe if I saw him, as Alma did, once every three years ..."

Doctor Maras didn't ask for details about those erotic obsessions, or why Alma was still interested in them, convinced that, so as not to exacerbate his pain, Carmen wouldn't tell him the truth. And so the shadows that his sister-in-law's words had cast in his mind became much more impressive that night than the reality they reflected, and around eleven o'clock, unable to toss and turn in the bed any more, he dressed without a sound and went to find the sex maniac who had dared to kiss the boss's daughter at an age and a time when boys and girls would blush even if their shadows touched.

12

HE DID NOT have to look for very long. There were only two restaurants in the harbour, one of them called Chez René.

Nor did he have to search for his wife's first lover. Like the harbour, the restaurant was plunged in darkness and silence, but its owner was sitting on his terrace, gazing at a freighter flying the Norwegian flag, the only one docked at the wharf.

The two men had only met once, some twenty years earlier. Since then, René Poitras had gotten so fleshy and was now so unlike the image he had kept of him that Doctor Maras wouldn't have recognized him if the restaurateur, seeing him, hadn't struggled out of his chair to offer—along with the foul stench of beer on his breath—his condolences. He looked so morose, Doctor Maras assumed that he too was grieving for Alma until the other man, in the same tone and with no transition, gestured vaguely towards the Norwegian freighter, saying:

"I waited all evening for a sailor to come down for a

drink and offer me the charity of a kiss. They've got such muscles, their armpits are the only tender part where I could put my hand to fall asleep afterwards."

Doctor Maras thought: What an idiot I am! He's gay and ever since the kiss he'd exchanged with Alma he'd assumed his homosexuality, and his erotic obsessions that gave my wife such a good laugh were only about men.

Relieved, he explained to René Poitras why he had come to La Malbaie.

"La Malbaie for all eternity?" René Poitras snickered. "Did Alma have that many sins to atone for? Now Doctor, I'm not saying she wasn't happy here. But La Malbaie for her was nothing more than a family album that she opened once every three or four years. Her first school. Her first communion. Her first kiss. And the boy who gave it to her had turned queer. Even the theatre where she performed isn't there any more."

"The summer theatre isn't there now?"

"The government took it over and turned it into a casino. That's why Alma gave an interview to the *Journal de Charlevoix*. To help the company get another space. Didn't Carmen tell you?"

"No."

"She was probably afraid you wouldn't bring the ashes ... Don't be mad at her. She's getting old and she wants so badly to have a man to think about. A decent man. There are so few around here ... In fact, aside from beer and slot machines there isn't much of anything. And Carmen rarely drinks and she hates gambling. Even

Alma, the last time she came here, she suffocated, the way I suffocate twelve months of the year, and all she talked about was Montreal, Paris, the Aegean Sea …"

Recollecting the Aegean Sea reminded the restaurateur of the Norwegian ship. He returned his gaze to it and said:

"Ah, to bind his feet and wrists to the bars of his berth …"

But there wasn't a living soul on the wharf, no one on the deck of the ship, only subdued light at two portholes.

"Maybe I should take a case of beer and knock on one of the portholes …"

"That's what I'd do."

"Do you think they'll want someone old and fat and ugly like I am now?"

This time Doctor Maras did not reply. Even sober, René Poitras must be very garrulous when the conversation had to do with him and his obsessions, and he'd only brought up the portholes to involve the doctor, as he must have done with Alma, in the delirium of his frustrations and his fantasies. Doctor Maras was quick then to hold out his hand, which the other man clasped reluctantly, saying:

"You should take the ashes to Paris."

"Why?"

"Alma dreamed of being buried in Père-Lachaise."

"She never told me that."

"She couldn't, Doctor. How could she have confessed without upsetting you that her time in France had been the most exciting period of her life, the time when she had tasted happiness most fully? Even on stage, so she said, she'd never given herself so completely. And every night, after every performance, before the sweet waves of applause from the Parisian audience, she felt that she could fly higher, ever higher."

13

AH, ALMA, IF there is life after life and the dead can observe the living, how you must regret your last wish!

You told your beloved husband: You will put my ashes in the place where I was happiest.

Since then there has been neither peace nor rest for him; he is constantly searching for that place. And just as he thought that he'd finally found it, he learns that he has slipped up again.

Do you see how laboriously he plods up the steep and winding road from the harbour to your childhood home? Can you make out in the darkness the distress in which you have sunk him? Can you hear how, word by word, he exhumes from his memory the account you had given him of your first visit to Paris, two years before your marriage, when you acted at the Théâtre national de Chaillot, with your friend Pauline Brunet?

"I was young and fresh and as lovely as a flower," you had told him. "*Paris Match* had devoted two pages to me. People turned around to look at me on the street. Waiters in cafés smiled at me. And in the theatre the director, Serge Groslin, hung around me like a lovelorn boy. Once, during a run-through, he jumped onto the stage and told me: 'You are mine tonight or I'll kill myself!' But I didn't give in. I'd heard it said that before opening night he got it off with all the new actresses he worked with and forgot them as soon as he was into a new project."

Yes, that's exactly what you'd told him.

And yet shortly after your wedding you went back to France where Groslin's first film was being shot. And in the darkness that has covered his world, your Alexandre is wondering now if it is possible that the twenty-four years you spent with him had mattered less for you than those two brief stays in France when you were starting out.

Rather than let his imagination get carried away again, he leaves a note for Carmen, then gets back on the road to Montreal. And at the first red glimmer of dawn, as soon as he'd arrived at the house, being careful not to waken Mélissa, he goes through your papers for some clue that would confirm or contradict that new doubt, and he digs out six photos taken at Père-Lachaise: two of you looking at Molière's grave, one at Jim Morrison's, another at Édith Piaf's, a fifth at Sarah Bernhardt's and finally, you and Pauline at the columbarium, in front of the immense wall that holds the remains of a thousand more celebrities.

What should he deduce from that?

He is scrutinizing them again, as if the photos could speak, when Mélissa gets up. And when he tells her of his meeting with René Poitras, she blows up for the first time since you died.

"Honestly, papa, I hardly recognize you. You've been telling me for years not to trust hypotheses with no basis in fact, to always be sure that there's tangible proof, a diagnostic sign, before drawing a conclusion, and here you are all shaken up by something you're told by a drunk. And a frustrated old queen on top of it. Did René at least tell you when Mama confessed that she wanted to be buried at Père-Lachaise? No? I'm not surprised. He saw Mama once every three years. How could he remember when she'd mentioned Père-Lachaise? If you ask me it must have been after her first trip to Paris, before she met you. And those photos confirm it: Pauline wasn't there on the second trip. And it's normal that, at the age she was then, Mama would have dreamed of being buried at Père-Lachaise. Every young artist passing through Paris dreams of being buried among all those celebrities. Then they go home and forget it. You want proof? Never in my whole life have I heard Mama mention Père-Lachaise!"

Mélissa's way of thinking is logical, coherent, but he's still not convinced. And when his daughter shuts herself away in the bathroom for her shower, he looks up Serge Groslin's number in your address book and calls him at home, in Paris.

The director's wife, the actress Ninon Conti, answers.

"You're calling from Montreal?" she says. "Is that where you met my husband? He was there three months ago."

Your Alexandre is so surprised at this last remark that for a moment he can't say a word.

"It's my wife and him who were old friends," he manages to say at last.

"They're not now?"

"My wife passed away two weeks ago."

Ninon Conti offers her condolences, philosophizes a little about the ephemeral, then promises to tell her husband about your death.

"He'll want to offer you his condolences. What number should he call?"

"Don't bother, I'll call again."

And he hangs up, poor man—can you see him?—he hangs up, shaken.

14

NO ONE KNOWS what a day just beginning holds in store for us—Doctor Maras has had more than one proof of that in recent days—but this one, really, came out of the blue. And before he lets himself get carried away by another swirl of conjecture, he finds his wife's date book, reads the March pages one by one, and on the eighth finds a note written at two p.m. which gives him the strange impression that he has suddenly become the witness to his own life: Groslin/Sheraton.

"Why didn't you say anything?" he asks, his voice cracking with emotion. "You gave me detailed accounts of the rehearsals for Bernarda Alba, the divorce of one actress, another's facelift. Why didn't you say anything about your appointment with Groslin?"

He calls his wife's agent, Aline Diamond.

"Do you know Serge Groslin?"

"I know his films. Actually, he was in Montreal a few months ago to promote his latest. Alma must have mentioned it."

"All I know is that they saw one another ..."

"Surely she was going to tell you more when the contract was signed. Actors are so superstitious."

"Groslin had offered her work?"

"Yes, the lead in his next film."

Hanging up, Doctor Maras says:

"For months, years, you suffered because you weren't working and I moved heaven and earth to console you, calm you, cheer you up. So that theatre people wouldn't forget you I went with you to boring social events so that you'd go out and they would see you. All of a sudden you're offered the lead in a film but you couldn't share that good news with me? Why?"

Unable to sit still he paces the room, plunges again into the labyrinths of memory, rehashes his thoughts, develops new hypotheses, turns the elements over in every direction, more and more surprised to be talking to himself.

"It couldn't be superstition. You told me everything, to get my opinion. About every person you called. Every step you took. Why didn't you tell me about Groslin? And if he offered you a part, why didn't he tell his wife? She didn't seem to know you when I spoke to her. And why didn't he say that he'd seen you in Montreal? Was Groslin superstitious too?"

It was as if he were spinning his wheels.

"If only you'd mentioned it!"

When his daughter gets out of the shower and invites him to have breakfast with her, he is in such a state he can't even drink his coffee.

"Don't tell me you're thinking about René Poitras again!" Mélissa exclaims.

He tells her about his phone call to Paris, his conversation with Aline Diamond.

"So?" his daughter says. "Mama called everybody for work. When she found out that Groslin was in Montreal she contacted him too."

"Why didn't she say anything to me? She used to tell me everything ..."

"Maybe she thought you'd object to her working with Groslin."

"Because he'd been chasing her twenty-five years ago? She went back to work with him after we were married."

"So why such a fuss about it now?"

They were going in circles and instead of continuing like that, inflicting on his child his own doubts and concerns in addition to her grief, he decides to get some fresh air, taking with him the business card the clairvoyant had left him.

15

WHEN MADAME ÉLIAS saw the look on his face, she asked, concerned, how he felt.

For the first time in his life, Doctor Maras replied: "Old."

The woman raised her right index finger, the bracelets that covered her arm jangling.

"Tsk, tsk, don't ever say you feel old. You must say that you feel you're becoming wiser."

He snickered, then asked the clairvoyant if Alma had ever talked about her plans.

"Sorry, everything that's said within these four walls is confidential."

"I have to know. Alma asked me to scatter her ashes in the place where she was happiest but she never said where that was. I wanted to bury her ashes in our garden. Is that the wrong place? Am I deluding myself? Is it pretentious of me to think that her private happiness was limited to me? You have to help me find the answer. You're my last hope."

Madame Élias thought for a moment, then said:

"I know a way that will satisfy your curiosity and preserve my integrity. Let me collect my thoughts and Alma will tell me everything you need to know."

Doctor Maras was a man of a gentle nature who always spoke in the same calm tone he used when speaking with a patient. This time, he who even as a child had only twice raised his hand to someone and that was to defend his sister, was, as they say, foaming with rage. With flames shooting from his eyes, he said:

"Do you take me for an idiot?"

"No ..."

"Then don't talk to me about communicating with Alma or I'll stuff your bracelets down your throat."

Madame Élias began to tremble.

"To tell you the truth," she said, "your wife sensed that *Bernarda Alba* would be her swan song, the end of the dream, and she regretted that she hadn't stayed in France where actresses of her age are still valued. So when she told me that Groslin was in Montreal I advised her to call him, especially because I could see in the cards a change in her destiny and that her life was approaching an important turn. 'Right now you can change the star that governs your career,' I told her. And I wasn't mistaken: Groslin offered her a role in his next film. As a result the future was smiling on her again, as it had when she was taking her first steps as an actress, when Groslin had opened to her the gates of happiness and fame. I'm not saying that she was unhappy with you. She quite simply needed to make a choice: to bow to the destiny that age had in store for her or expatriate herself to work and dream again. But she didn't know how to tell you that and she kept putting off the moment, because she loved you. I swear that on the lives of my children Alma loved you very much and she told me again and again that you were the best of husbands."

But Doctor Maras was already heading for the exit and he had stopped listening.

16

WHEN HE GOT home it seemed as if the flowers his wife had planted in the garden had rushed into bloom, opening to taunt him. When he finally went to bed that night, he felt the way he had as a child waiting for sleep, trying in the dark to imagine where the universe begins and where it ends.

But on waking he'd made up his mind: He would go to Paris and talk to Serge Groslin face-to-face. He made a reservation on a plane departing the next evening and called his secretary to let her know. As well, he phoned his sister in Paris to tell her that he would arrive on Sunday and asked her to make an appointment with Groslin for him on Monday. But not at his place: He didn't want to talk about Alma in the presence of his wife.

"Do you really have to?" his sister asked. "Aren't you going a bit too far?"

"In every image in my mind Alma and I are together. How could I go on living with those images while doubting the emotions they express?"

"All right, okay, I'll call Groslin."

When it's Mélissa's turn to get up, he asks her to take care of her mother's garden while he's away.

"There's always the hope that she'll come back with me," he says, struggling to put a smile in his voice.

To his great surprise, this time his daughter does not try to hold him back or make him change his mind. On the contrary, she approves of his decision as if, seeing him so overwhelmed by doubt these past few days, she couldn't ask him to doubt the rest of his life.

"She'll come back," she says quite simply, "and we'll be able finally to live our mourning in peace."

He feels bad at having again forgotten that Mélissa is grieving too and that once more he will be leaving her alone with her grief. To redeem himself, he promises her that after his return on Tuesday, whether he comes back with or without the ashes, he'll talk to her only about the future. And the next day, before he leaves for the airport, he calls his daughter's boyfriend to ask him to take care of her while he is away.

"It would be better for Mélissa not to spend those three days alone."

"Why? What did she tell you?"

"What do you mean, why? She's just lost her mother! Should there be something else?"

"No, no," the other man replies hastily, as if sorry he'd asked the question. "There's nothing else."

Doctor Maras is not convinced and wants to make him say more, but his taxi has arrived.

The driver is one of his patients, Abdo Adaïmi, a Lebanese in his fifties who has congenital glaucoma and whose taxi always smells of mandarins or oranges. Abdo doesn't know that his eye-doctor has lost his wife and, seeing his grim expression, he tells him a story to amuse him.

"Remember my associate, Georges Boutros, Doctor? Twenty-five years ago, during the war in Lebanon, he was clubbed in his left eye and you took out the cataract that developed there."

"Yes, I remember him."

"He's in jail."

"Why?"

"A couple of months ago he picked up a fare who wanted to go to the corner of Monkland and Royal, in Notre-Dame-de-Grâce. When he realized that Georges was Lebanese too, he started telling him that he was going to get it off with a married woman he'd met in a bar where she hung out when her husband was at work. She wasn't hot but she was submissive and compliant, he said ... You hear these things in a taxi, Doctor ... You have no idea what tales our fares tell us. At first, Georges only half-listened. But the more the guy said about what he was going to do to the woman he was on his way to get it on with, the worse Georges felt for her and for her husband. Until they arrived at the corner of Monkland and Royal. The guy paid Georges, with a tip as big as the prospect of the pleasures he was going to experience, then he got out. But Georges didn't leave. He lived in the same neighbourhood and he wanted to see which of his neighbours' houses the guy would go into. And what doorbell do you think he saw Casanova ring?"

He laughed.

"I tell you, Doctor, there are coincidences that make a man really believe in the existence of Satan ..."

Doctor Maras did not laugh at all. In fact, if Abdo Adaïmi wanted to cheer him up he'd only managed to make him gloomier. And now it was with a sombre face that, as soon as he was buckled into his seat, he asked the flight attendant not to let anyone wake him up before arrival, then he gulped a sleeping pill to give himself a rest from his thoughts.

17

HE LANDED AT Charles de Gaulle on Sunday morning. Hélène and her husband, director of photography Franck Rondot, had the day off and had come to meet him.

In the car, Hélène informed her brother that she'd made an appointment for him with Serge Groslin on Tuesday afternoon.

"Why not tomorrow?"

"He left for Marseille yesterday and won't be back till noon on Tuesday."

He was going to stew in doubt for another day and just thinking about it made him choke. Hélène knew that and it pained her to see her brother so broken. But she also knew that only Groslin could take him out of the abyss into which Alma's last wishes had cast him and said nothing.

Franck was driving.

Suddenly he said:

"If it was me, instead of torturing myself I'd go and find that son of a bitch's wife."

Doctor Maras did not react.

Neither did his sister.

Franck raised his voice.

"Groslin must've told his wife about whatever feelings Alma still had for him, even if it was just to brag. I know him."

The other two still said nothing.

Franck glanced in the rearview mirror.

"If you're afraid of confronting his wife, I'll go with you."

"I'll wait till Tuesday," Doctor Maras finally said.

"Do you think Groslin will tell you the truth? Coward that he is, he'll be super careful not to reveal anything for fear that you'll smash his face. And that scum won't just take the mickey out of you. What a great idea for a film, he'll say, a guy looks for the place where his beloved was the happiest to scatter her ashes. And as soon as you're gone, he'll jot down everything you told him to pass on to his buddies or use in a film, never overburdening himself with scruples as you do."

"Maybe so. I'm still waiting till Tuesday."

Franck turned towards his wife.

"They're something else, these Canadians, eh? He's been given horns and he'd rather mope and feel sorry for himself than upset the wife of the guy that cuckolded him. Finally I understand why you've turned out as many great men as we've produced seal hunters."

Hélène observed her husband for a moment.

"You seem to be mad at Groslin."

"I'm just trying to help your brother. Obviously, even though he's a doctor he doesn't know what cowardice can lead to. At first, it seems easy. You invent a thousand reasons for not putting your words into action. But you always pay the price in the end. Pimples, ulcers, insomnia, cancer ..."

18

FRANK WOULDN'T LET the matter go. While Doctor Maras settled into the guest room, washed, and called his daughter to tell her he'd be coming home a day later, his brother-in-law, an assiduous reader of scholarly works as well as fiction, consulted several in search of arguments that would help him convince his guest to go and see Ninon Conti. And at dinner that night, all puffed up with his finds, he asked:

"What is happiness, Alexandre? What in your opinion is the meaning of that word?"

Because of jet lag, fatigue, and his torments, Doctor Maras had trouble focusing his thoughts and, caught off guard, he spluttered.

Franck burst out laughing.

"You're hilarious! You're trying to find the place where your wife was happiest and you don't know the meaning of the word?"

"You aren't going to start bugging him again with that," Hélène said.

"Feeling his pain won't lighten his suffering," her

husband replied. "As long as we're at it why not drive nails into his hands and pour him some vinegar to quench his thirst?"

Then he launched into an exposition that quickly revealed the extent of his knowledge both general and specific.

Reduced to silence by his brother-in-law's verbal avalanche, Doctor Maras, whenever an argument came to the tip of his tongue to defend the happiness he had experienced so often when he was back home with his wife and his daughter, for example, after a good day's work, he would think to himself: That's too superficial, and choke it back. Hence, when his sister finally asked her husband if one had to conclude that happiness on earth is a figment of the imagination, even if his whole body wanted to cry out No, he waited for Franck's reply with the expression his patients wore when they were waiting for his diagnosis.

"*Happiness is merely an idea*," Franck read in a psychiatry text. "*Only pleasure is concrete, as is displeasure. And one of the most complex and most interesting points in psychiatry is the coexistence of pleasure and pain. Masochism is the most obvious form of that state.*"

Doctor Maras protested:

"I came to Paris out of duty."

Franck turned toward his wife and, savouring every word, said to her:

"Typical reply of a masochist, like the saint or the soldier who devote themselves to a noble cause, regardless of the danger and pain involved. And Alma, knowing her husband's sense of duty, arranged through her last wishes to make him pay for all the years she'd devoted to him rather than to her career."

Doctor Maras protested again. Yes, he said, like everyone else Alma had her faults and she could occasionally be nasty, especially when she heard the excessive flattery that less talented actresses received for roles that she was no longer offered. She could also prove to be jealous and possessive, especially when she saw the way young women made eyes at her husband. But never, ever had she in a calculating way caused harm to another. "What is it about young girls?" she said quite simply. "To keep in shape they just have to flutter their eyelashes." Yes, she had humour and wit, even if she preferred to play tragic roles. Alma also had a big heart, even when it was at its sickest.

Franck looked his brother-in-law up and down with an appearance of pity.

"She had a big heart ... Of course, you know everything that was in it. You would swear to it, wouldn't you? Either you're more naïve than I thought or you'd circumvent the truth to spare your memories and go on deluding yourself. Goddammit! Put aside your emotions as if you were treating a patient, and just think about yourself for once. What do we know in actual fact about the hearts of others, Alexandre? Really? What do we know about the hearts of others aside from what they want us to see? Alma was intending to leave you. Had she told you? No. And because death would prevent her from coming to Paris and whereas you had a strong, dependable heart and were going to stay alive to enjoy it, she thought up those last wishes to piss you off from her funeral up until yours. That's possible, isn't it?"

Doctor Maras suddenly recalled what Nicole Gouin had said to Pauline Brunet: The only times she would see Alma happy were when she was pissing everybody off, and with her last wishes she pissed off everyone even after her death.

"Anything's possible," he said finally.

Franck put his hand on the hand of Doctor Maras.

"If you don't want Alma's so-called happiness to become your hell, at least have the balls to dig up some courage and see Ninon Conti tomorrow. She's the only one who will tell you the truth. She'll even help you pay back her bastard of a husband for his treachery, if you tell her that he intended to give Alma a role that he hadn't offered to her first."

Doctor Maras, whom wine made more nostalgic than aggressive, recalled two verses by Racine that he'd learned back in the days when he helped his wife to memorize her lines and said:

> *Too long I've shown you love's violence*
> *To lapse into a dull indifference.*

Franck took away his hand.

"People are pissing you off and you laugh?"

"Leave him alone and think, will you?" Hélène told her husband. "A woman of Alma's age doesn't cross out a marriage with a stroke of a pen overnight. She doesn't even want to look any more, all she desires is to keep what she has."

Franck shook his head.

"Alma was above all an actress. And I know a good number of actresses. I've worked with hundreds over the past forty years. They have an unhealthy need to be loved. And not just by their spouses. That's why their careers always set the tone for every step they take, for all their relationships. The situation is even worse for actresses whose age has reduced their charm and their power of seduction. So any trick, any lie, and every form of cruelty are considered to be totally fair. Especially if Groslin had held out the possibility of a role that would have rebooted her career in Paris and taken her to the top again."

"And why would Groslin do that?" Hélène asked.

"Maybe Ninon Conti doesn't indulge his every whim."

"That's hogwash. Men Groslin's age are interested mainly in fresh young meat that gives them the illusion of potency. Why would he bring here from Montreal a woman older than his own wife when Paris is overflowing with young things who'd be prepared to go down the Champ-Élysées on their hands and knees to nab a bit part?"

"Some men have perversions that not many women will submit to, especially Frenchwomen. And Groslin, from what people say, likes watching two chicks tickle one another."

Hélène bursts out laughing.

"Now you're delirious for sure. But what did Groslin do to you to make you go so far as to soil Alma's memory and destroy the peace of her household?"

Doctor Maras wasn't laughing now. He rose abruptly from the table and said:

"I'm wiped out. Please excuse me, I'm going to bed."

"Good idea!" his sister said.

19

IT WAS BECOMING harder and harder for him to get over jet lag and his face was puffy from fatigue. He had not retired to the guest room to lie down though. As soon as Franck had mentioned the sexual perversion of Serge Groslin, his mind had rewound to the Orphée theatre, more precisely, just as Nicole Gouin was telling Pauline Brunet to put dear Alma's ashes under her desk to have them always between her legs. And now, though he knew that one should beware of these associations of ideas, that the players in this game are nearly always wrong, he wondered for the first time in twenty-four years why his wife's best friend was a lesbian. And as happens at such moments, the more he wondered, the more his mind drifted towards trivial matters that now took on a totally new meaning, until everything that had seemed clear and solid to him now showed itself to be dark and slimy.

Even the most insignificant chatter.

Alma was rehearsing Medea. One day she was complaining about the actor playing Jason who was constantly changing his acting style, which unsettled her;

another day, she griped about the actor playing Creon, a skinflint, she claimed, who would hasten his own death to take advantage of a sale on coffins.

That night, Alma cursed the director who wanted to cut two of her lines.

"Medea exits once, intending to kill her children," she explained to her husband. "But though she's furious with Jason who has left her for a younger woman—she who abandoned family and homeland for him—she stops herself, comes back on stage and says: *My heart is water at the sight of my children's bright faces. I could never do it. No! I cannot do it.* But Euripides, who knew a thing or two about women, was well aware that the rejected spouse kills not so much from love as from wounded pride, then has her say: *What is the matter with me? Do I want to make myself a laughing-stock by letting my enemies off scot-free?* And it is then that she exits and slits her children's throats. She is fully aware of the reasons for her behaviour because she says: *Alas! My own pride has brought me to misery.* And that idiot wants to cut those two lines, cut her into a desperate dish rag, direct it for marshmallow-lovers because he can't imagine that a woman could also be proud and that her pride could be even more powerful than mother love!"

Today, Doctor Maras remembers all that and wonders if Franck may have been right to say that Alma, embittered by her woes, had arranged, in a final act of revenge, to make her own presumed happiness her husband's misery. Not only had he forced her to leave the suburbs for the city—she who had sacrificed a career in

France to return to her own country's wide open spaces —his wife's face was now twice as wrinkled as his own, though she was four years younger, and every morning in front of her mirror complained that it was harder and harder to stick all the pieces together.

He obviously just had to set out onto that trail and memory, implacable tyrant, would start to collect and to misrepresent any number of clues to feed the voracious appetite for bitterness. And as everyone knows, when memory wakens, forget about sleep.

20

HE DOES NOT take a sleeping pill though and, the next day, his eyes are smarting when he goes into the Air France office to change his return date. Stopping along the way at the Théâtre national de Chaillot where, according to Alma, Groslin had lurked around her like a lovelorn boy. But she had not given in. Which was what she had told him and he'd believed her, though she had also said that you have to be something of a whore in her line of work.

Idiot! he thinks to himself now. Would Groslin have re-engaged her?

After he's changed his return date, he goes to the 6th arrondissement, to the Hôtel Saint-André-des-Arts where Alma had stayed the first time she had worked in Paris. Like the Théâtre national de Chaillot, the hotel is unchanged since the days some years later when Alma had brought her husband there to show it to him.

She had told him:

"Pauline was in the cast and she stayed here too. At night, when we came back from the theatre we'd stop at the gelateria on rue de Buci for an ice cream cone before we went up to bed. You must try it, Alexandre, it's the best in the world."

The gelateria is still there, fifty metres away. But when Doctor Maras sits down at the café across the street, instead of seeing Alma and Pauline lined up for a cone after a performance, he sees them going directly up to their room on the arms of Serge Groslin.

He isn't angry with her for that: He and Alma hadn't met yet. He is angry with her for having hidden from him that she loved Groslin and having returned to Paris two years after their marriage to perform in his first feature film.

Come to think of it, even when she was working outside of Montreal she would call him every night to tell him about her day, imagining like all actors that the entire world would find it fascinating. But though he searches his memory he can't find the slightest reference to Groslin's first film. Why? Was she who lied so badly in real life afraid of giving away her feelings? Unless she was much less honest than she seemed and only revealed to him certain fragments of what she did and thought, which amounts to a kind of lie, doesn't it?

All things considered, Franck was right: The woman whose table and bed he had shared for twenty-four years had never truly opened the doors to her heart, never truly let him into her other garden, the secret one. It was as though her status as spouse were merely another role she was playing, and today he chokes at the thought that every time she looked at him she could tell herself: You can see me, hear me, you can even enter my body but never will you be able to enter my mind.

Perhaps if he didn't go to bed so early at night ...

Alma always came home from performances overcharged and needing to talk while he, as a surgeon, had to get up every morning at five o'clock, perfectly rested.

How she must have missed while he was snoring not being with someone in her line of work, like Groslin, who'd have taken her for an ice cream after the theatre and listened to her recount her joys and anxieties all night ...

He looks back at the gelateria across the street and now sees a mockery in every detail, from its name, Amorino, to the little cupid that symbolized its products, even in the way of eating the cones.

"I wanted so badly for my sister to see Paris too," says an American woman at the next table.

"Why didn't she come with you?" asks her female companion.

"She can't, poor thing, her husband is still alive."

Doctor Maras pays his bill and walks away, head bowed, and after walking for an hour ends up at Père-Lachaise cemetery where, with a map in hand and a lump in his throat, he visits the graves of Jim Morrison, Molière, Sarah Bernhardt and Edith Piaf, ending up at the columbarium, convinced that Groslin himself had photographed Alma and Pauline here and that on that day he and Alma had sworn to join each other there for eternity. And tomorrow, the director was going to confirm it to him.

Fortunately, he still has Mélissa.

Unless ...

A thought takes hold of him, one of those thoughts that break a man for life. To check it, he takes out his pen and jots two dates on the back of his plane ticket so he can accurately calculate the number of months between Alma's return from Paris after shooting Groslin's first film and the birth of their daughter.

"Watch out, Monsieur," shouts a teenager passing by with his buddies. "Every year a hundred people choke to death on their pens."

His friends split their sides laughing. In other circumstances, Doctor Maras would have laughed too. This time, he rushes to the exit, gasping for breath even though he's in the open air.

When he is finally back at his sister's, no sooner has he crossed the threshold than Franck returns to the attack.

"So, Ninon Conti? Did you go?"

"No."

"What a masochist!"

Doctor Maras nods, then shuts himself inside the guest room.

The urn sits on the bedside table. He looks at it and has the impression that he is gazing at the ashes of his life.

21

BE BRAVE, HE tells himself on Tuesday, as he leaves his sister's apartment. You must learn to accept things as they are. Nothing lasts forever. Be brave, he tells himself again as he enters the café where Serge Groslin is waiting for him, tanned, alert, and as slim and graceful at sixty as a young tennis champion. Surely, he thinks, Mélissa would be more proud of a father so handsome, so talented, so famous ...

"Doctor, my deepest sympathy."

Doctor Maras thanks him, then explains without further ado why he has come to Paris.

"How touching," Groslin says. "To look for the place where one's beloved has been happiest and leave her ashes there. And you didn't tell my wife on the phone to spare me. Your kindness touches me deeply. But I assure you, between Alma and me there was only friendship. And on my part, tremendous admiration for her talent, her intelligence and that rare and magical gift of hers: presence. For her courage too. Because it takes courage and great strength of character when, after people have praised you to the skies, they turn their backs on you. And so when I found out in Montreal that she was no longer working, I didn't hesitate to offer her a part in my upcoming film."

"When was it going to be shot?"

"Next spring."

He's not even surprised that I don't know, thinks Doctor Maras as Groslin shakes his head and says:

"What a pity. She was wild about the subject too because she thought it was unacceptable that in the twenty-first century, the past could still poison our present and threaten our future as it is doing in so many countries. That must stop. People should learn once and for all that we cannot advance by constantly looking back. Otherwise I feel sorry for children in the year 3000 who'll have another thousand years of resentments to deal with."

Why is he telling him all that? Doctor Maras knows, from having lived with an actress and become familiar with her circles, those people get carried away easily and can talk about the project they're working on as if it were the most fascinating thing in the world. But Groslin puts too much emphasis on the words *past* and *stop* for it to be idle chatter. Doctor Maras lets him hold forth then on the different theatres of war and extermination throughout the world, analyzing every one of his sentences, every intonation. But despite his seeming affability, the other man is still vague and Doctor Maras is no further ahead when Groslin has finished demonstrating that the most highly developed countries are those that pay the least tribute to the past. Now, his tirade finished, he looks at his watch and asks for the bill. Doctor Maras concludes then that the man has told him everything that had driven him to write his screenplay, either to point out, without taunting him, that the world was being torn apart by war and there was no reason to be troubled over a personal drama so insignificant compared with those of thousands of other people, or quite simply to prevent him from asking questions, and now he was going to dash on the pretext that more important matters awaited him.

As it happens, Groslin is already getting to his feet, pretending to be sorry he couldn't stay longer.

But Doctor Maras doesn't let himself be thrown. He looks the director in the eye and says:

"You may have finished with the past but the past hasn't finished with me. If you don't want it to poison my future, tell me, in your soul and conscience: Where should I leave Alma's ashes?"

Groslin shrugs.

"I don't even know what was the happiest point of my own life. In France, some cemeteries reserve a corner for a memorial garden, where people can scatter the ashes of their dead and come back to visit them, like a grave. For me, all of Paris, all of France, the entire planet have become my memorial garden. Because every time I think that I've found that moment of fullness in one place, I recall ten more that are engraved in my memory and are equally dazzling."

I should have gone to see his wife, thinks Doctor Maras, as the other man exclaims:

"Oh, I nearly forgot ..."

He takes two folded sheets of paper from his pocket.

"I got this letter two weeks ago. I reread it before I came here and I thought that you'd like to have it."

He glances again at his watch.

"One last question. Do you remember in what month you shot your film with Alma, twenty-two years ago?"

Serge Groslin reflects for a moment, then says:

"July. I remember because we'd shot one scene during the Bastille Day celebrations."

It wasn't nine months as he had thought but eleven months before Mélissa's birth. Still, after Groslin left, he hesitates for a long moment before he unfolds the paper, as if his entire past depended on their contents. His future too.

22

THE DATE ON the letter was the one when Alma had learned that she had to have surgery, and her long, slanted handwriting, usually so clear, was forced, jittery, agitated.

Dear Serge,

You can't imagine how thrilled I was at the prospect of working with you again—and in front of the camera. Unfortunately, it won't be possible: a narrowing of my aortic valve is so advanced that I'm to have emergency surgery the day after tomorrow. Even if I survive, the convalescence will take months, if not years. In case my heart packs it in, before I go I want to thank you for your offer and your friendship.

These past few days I've often wondered what kind of career I'd have had if I had slept with all the directors who wanted me. After all, we have just one life and my life has taught me that what's important is not what we deserve but what we are bold enough to take. But I soon console myself with the thought that, unlike lots of actresses who think about nothing but their career, I will grow old with a man who loves me and whom I adore and a daughter who will give me even more joy when she gives me grandchildren.

Laugh if you want at my lack of ambition but on the eve of my surgery I have just one regret: not seeing Paris one last time and most of all, the island of Leros in the Aegean Sea where, with Alexandre and Mélissa who was still a child, I spent the most beautiful two months of my life, thinking about nothing except enjoying this world and its light. After our shoot next year I intended to bring them there. It would have been my surprise gift for our silver wedding. But if I wake up from my operation the day after tomorrow, I will ask my husband to take me there as soon as I can travel. I doubt that Mélissa will want to come. She has other fish to fry this summer. If she could talk about it with her father I wouldn't worry. But she doesn't dare tell him that medicine bores her for fear of letting him down.

Pray for me. Three more months of grace, three more months of life, to see Paris and Leros again, and above all to look after my little darling who is suffering right now the way we suffer at her age when we don't know what it is we want from life.

My very best to Ninon.
Love,
Alma

23

FOR A LONG moment he stared at the two sheets of paper and saw again his final image of her: Alma at the very moment of orgasm, murmuring Yes, yes, and then expiring.

Half an hour later he changed his return date for Montreal once again and bought a ticket for Athens. There was an airport on the island of Leros now but he decided to go there by boat as he'd done with Alma and Mélissa sixteen years before.

"Well?" Franck asked when Doctor Maras returned to his sister's place to pack. "Was I right? You should have talked to Ninon Conti?"

"No. Alma told me everything I wanted to know."

Hélène was still at work and he told her on the phone that he was leaving that same evening.

"If only she'd told me that it was in Leros ..."

"You'd have concluded that, ever since then, she'd never been so happy with you."

"That's true ..."

"You have to think about yourself now, Alex. A dead

woman, no matter how much you've loved her, is no companion for a living man."

Doctor Maras also called home to tell Mélissa that he would be delayed again.

"Are you relieved?" his daughter asked. "You won't be coming home with the ashes but at least it will be settled; you won't have to look any more."

"Yes, I'm better now. What about you? How are you?"

"I'm trying to get used to the fact that I'll never see her again."

"Aside from that?"

"Looking after the garden ..."

Should he mention her studies and what Alma had said in her letter? He'd had a first sign in Saint-Hilaire when Mélissa had told Zak she envied artists because they didn't have to worry about their future, it was all mapped out by their talent. He had intended to talk with her about it when they were back at the house but Carmen's letter had prevented it and he was travelling again while his child was overwhelmed by her grief and, as well, by all her doubts about her choice of career. Even now, he hesitated to broach the subject because he preferred to talk about such important matters face-to-face rather than on the phone. And while he was still hesitating Mélissa said:

"When you've finished in Greece, call and let me know when your plane gets in. I'll pick you up at the airport."

"Okay. Would you like something from Leros?"

"A wave."

He smiled.

"I love you, papa."

He was annoyed with himself for not having said it first and when, in a flood of tenderness he finally replied, Mélissa had hung up.

24

GREECE: A UNIGUE EXPERIENCE.

The poster hangs above the carousel where passengers on the flight from CDG-Paris are waiting to retrieve their baggage. It shows a young couple embracing on a golden sand beach.

It has been years since Doctor Maras has looked at his photos from Greece. Had he known he would end up there he'd have brought one to better recall what Alma looked like that summer when death, for her, was merely a notion as abstract as the horizon.

"Excuse me, Madame," a woman behind him says to another. "You've taken my suitcase."

Doctor Maras looks at the conveyor belt and, when he realizes that half the suitcases filing past look like his, he starts running left and right to check the label on each one that resembles his which the passengers take off the carousel. He looks ridiculous, he knows it, but he doesn't want someone else inadvertently leaving with Alma's ashes, especially because it's nearly midnight and everyone is anxious to go to bed. When he finally picks up his suitcase, he doesn't let go of it, especially on the ferry for the island of Leros that he takes the next morning at the port of Piraeus.

The crossing takes eleven hours and the smells, the sounds, the commotion surrounding him, from the stampede of passengers toward the best seats to the long lines in front of the bar, recall a flock of images that come with no need for him to summon up a memory. Especially of the sky that in the past he would see every morning, equally pure and luminous, and the sea that made a person want to dream. And so he stays on the bridge, sitting on a bench with his suitcase at his feet, looking now at the traces of foam that the boat leaves behind, now at the gulls that follow the wake, now the islands and rocks that appear then disappear, just as a group of Japanese seniors block his view to have their pictures taken against the ship's rail with, in the background, a huge incandescent sun sinking into the horizon.

A young Frenchman siting on the same bench with his girlfriend says to her:

"Why are they taking photos? They've got one foot in the grave!"

In the dining room he shares a table with an English tourist around his age and the only passenger who is not watching the television screens where in every corner one can see Redskins tying a missionary to a tree and saying to him: "If faith can move mountains, move that one!"

The Englishman chews slowly as he gazes at a postcard in front of his plate. It shows an ancient statue of a satyr with a lecherous smile, half-man, half-goat, with the beginnings of a potbelly, hooves, and an erection as long as his forearm.

"That's Silenus, chief of the satyrs," he explains to Doctor Maras. "Since life is what it is, if I had to give a human face to fate, I would choose Silenus. Look at him. His whole being reeks of irony. His smile. The way his left hand is placed on his hip. The way his right arm is raised. His erection. Standing as if giving the finger to all humanity. You bunch of suckers, it says. I don't give a fuck about your piddling feelings, your piddling hopes and crappy certainties."

He looks again at the postcard.

"I'm going to have it framed and put it on my desk."

Doctor Maras goes back out on deck, still holding his suitcase. He gazes first at the Milky Way that flows from one end of the sky to the other, then at the darkness of the sea, while the boat sails on towards the past, with Alma beside him and the sleeping Mélissa in her arms.

Forgive me for doubting your love. The thought of losing my memories too, of seeing them replaced by a knot of bitterness for the rest of my life had totally unsettled me.

He goes on talking to his wife and the wind answers him, its breath laden with increasing clarity of the scents of the island where Alma intended to go the next summer and of which he can now make out the silhouette. A mixture of thyme and oregano that sixteen years earlier had led Alma cry out triumphantly, Cock-a-doodle-doo! And a rooster had answered in the middle of the night. Then another and another like a choir chanting at the top of their lungs a welcome to the young woman full of such vitality that like the sun, she filled with life every space she entered. And for her, he wanted to waken the roosters as she had done, but as they approached the harbour, there were more and more people on the deck and out of a sense of propriety he worried again about his suitcase so he wouldn't lose it in the crush of passengers disembarking one after the other.

An hour later, he finally put down his suitcase in a hotel room in Alinda, the small town that hugs the shore of the bay of the same name.

He took out the urn, set it on the dressing table.

Here you are at last in the place where you were happiest. It seems a little strange to me, leaving your ashes on an island in the outer reaches of the Mediterranean where you lived for barely two months. But as Greece was a unique experience for you as well ...

25

IT WAS AN obsession with her. When she wasn't working or when the snow covered her garden and she had only house plants to water, Alma spent hours rummaging in flea markets. In time, she became acquainted with all the second-hand dealers in Montreal, such as Tassos, a Greek whose daughter wanted to study at the National Theatre School. Alma helped her prepare her audition and to thank her, Tassos offered her for an entire summer a house he had on the island of Leros.

"It's on a hill, barely three hundred metres from the beach, and its terrace looks out on one of the most beautiful bays in the Aegean sea. Take advantage of it before the tourists discover it and spoil that island too."

Sixteen years had gone by but Doctor Maras was sure that he would find the little house: He would just have to go up from the beach along the road they took to go swimming. The house—he still remembered—was on the right-hand side, surrounded by a small garden in which there was a well. And it was in that same garden that he intended to bury the ashes.

The next morning though, as he left the hotel after breakfast, he felt lost, so much had the village of Alinda been developed. Sixteen years earlier there were only two hotels and the houses were scattered tens of metres apart. Now there were eight hotels and as many new construction sites. A dozen bars as well, boutiques and two supermarkets, whereas to do their shopping back then, they had to travel four kilometres to the village of Platanos, the island's capital, at the other end of the bay. Also, the number of houses had tripled and from a distance, all these new villas surrounded by enormous bougainvillea concealed from him the little garden where in the shadow of a vine on a pergola, while Mélissa was napping, he and Alma studied—she her next role, he the two or three medical books that he'd brought.

Fortunately there was the sea to guide him and by following the coast, he finally located the road that went up to the house between two hedges of oleander. He had forgotten the oleander but when he spotted them another flood of images unfurled in his memory: Mélissa at five running ahead of him towards the water while the morning sun shone, already hot. Three hours later, she went back up the hill on her father's shoulders, exhausted.

Behind them, Alma stopped along the way to admire a plant she'd have liked to have in her garden, but that could not survive in the Canadian climate, or to study another one that she didn't know.

"I wonder what that is ..."

And he, as fascinated by botany as Alma by ophthalmology, could only enlighten her once in two months.

"Belladonna."

She looked at him, astonished, as the asphalt simmered under their feet.

"They extract atropine from it, an alkaloid that makes the pupils dilate."

"Really?"

"During the Renaissance ladies in Italy put it in their eyes to make the man they wanted to seduce think that it was he who was stimulating their pupils. The men were so flattered that they only had eyes for women with dilated pupils like the eyes of a fawn, and that's where the plant gets its name: beautiful woman."

Alma, who when she was acting in a film or on television, put drops of collyrium in her eyes to make them brighter, asked him:

"Could you bring me some atropine from the clinic? I'll use it on the next shoot, before a close-up."

And Mélissa, perched on her father's shoulders, added:

"Me too, I want some!"

At length he found the house, or rather the spot it had once occupied. Because the house where Alma, always the smart dresser, had spent two months wearing only shorts, T-shirts, and sandals, no longer existed. Nor did the garden where she, the self-confessed chatterbox, had spent hours without uttering a word. A clothing store now occupied the whole piece of land and had he not gone inside to make inquiries, he'd have thought that he'd come to the wrong place.

There was only one young woman in the store, busy arranging a display of brooches and pins.

"Yes, this is where Tassos' house used to be," she told him in English. "He left it to his children when he died and as Leros meant nothing to them they sold it to me. I had the house torn down and had this store built."

It had been years since he'd thought about Tassos' house, let alone about seeing it again one day. But when he found out that it was no longer there, he felt as if something was suddenly missing in the world and he hastened to get back on the road with the oleanders and to the shore where, while Alma was tanning in the sun, he had taught Mélissa to swim, to float on her back, and to dive.

"Papa, why does the sea taste like my tears when I cry? Papa, why is there an eye painted on both sides of the fishing boat? Papa, why do a man and a woman close their eyes when they kiss?"

She had even noticed that donkeys and horses had eyes on the sides of their heads and not on the front like cats and dogs.

"Why?"

She always came to him, confident that he would answer all her questions, fulfill all her expectations. And he was delighted to find in the eyes of his child this astonishment at the sight of small things that, as he aged, were no longer mysterious or interesting in his own eyes.

"Mama, why do birds sing? Other birds can't hear them, they haven't got ears."

As if only her mother could answer questions about voice and hearing.

Today, her interest in anatomy was waning. But this was not the time to think about that.

26

HE TOOK A chair on the terrace of a café at the water's edge, in the shade of a pine tree. The bay that stretched out in front of him was sparkling in the blazing sun. At the end of the bay, two hills rose up like two breasts, and in the valley between them stood the village of Platanos where they used to do their shopping. On the left breast, the Byzantine citadel of Kastro, which they had visited twice, rose up like a nipple.

Remember? We came here to eat on nights when the moon was full to watch it rise between the two breasts. Bare coloured light bulbs shone above the tables. One night you asked for them to be turned off for a few minutes for a better view of the moonrise. When it finally appeared, you were so stirred that you pulled off your dress and in your underwear dove into the path it had traced on the surface of the water all the way to our table. Come in, you cried. I hesitated to leave Mélissa alone. She's asleep, you shouted. And we won't be swimming all the way to Turkey!

He stared at the water for a long moment, while the

intermittent song of the cicadas reverberated amid the needles of the pine tree overhead.

I could easily leave your urn at the bottom of this bay, but the water is so clear that a swimmer would spot it ...

He brought his gaze back to terra firma.

How about the beach?

Alma adored lying in the sun and she could sunbathe all day. He enjoyed the sun, for the pleasure of sitting in the shade, of gazing at the play of light on the water or in the pine trees that lined the shore, and daydreaming —as much as one can daydream while watching a five-year-old at the water's edge.

This morning he didn't see a single child. It was June, school was not yet over. He saw no adults either, neither on the sand nor in the water. He was the only customer at the café, and on the road that hugged the shore, the only outsiders were a man in his sixties walking on the shady side and pushing a woman in a wheelchair, the same age as he, humming to her an old tune by Aznavour and farther away, a woman dressed all in white and wearing a broad straw hat, who was strolling toward him, her gaze going from one feature of the landscape to another. And it was not until she walked past the café that he recognized the fiftyish tourist he'd run into at breakfast in the hotel dining room. She recognized him too and gave him a smile, which he returned.

No, the beach is not a good idea. There are no swimmers now, but soon the schools will be closed, hundreds of children will be digging with their shovels in the sand. If not that, the waves would expose your urn one day.

The waitress finally arrived, handed him the menu with a smile, then left again.

So what do we do?

Just then he heard the slow chiming of a bell sounding the knell in the distance.

He said to himself: It's true—it's suddenly come back—there was a little cemetery not far from the house where we were living. For sure no one will build a store or a hotel there. I'll go this afternoon. They're probably burying someone right now.

He called the waitress and without looking at the menu, ordered fried calamari, a salad and a half-litre of retsina, like in the good old days, then luxuriated once more in the melancholy slide show of his memories. But once he'd been served, he barely touched what he ordered when he realized that from now on there would be no one to travel with, or even to share his meals.

27

THE ALINDA CEMETERY stretched over the side of the mountain, a hundred metres from the house where they had lived. It was a small cemetery surrounded by cypresses, tall and straight as church candles, which held some fifty graves as well as an ossuary. Near the entrance, a teen-age boy with tear-filled eyes was gazing at the photo of a young girl that adorned a brand new headstone. Farther away, sitting on a grave of which the marble bore the mark of several winters, an old lady was talking to the photo of an old man as if she were telling him: Yesterday we celebrated our grand-daughter's wedding. I hope that she'll be as happy with her husband as I was with you.

Doctor Maras was thinking: It's a magnificent view. You can see the bay, the place where Tassos' house was, the path we took to the beach, the little café where we waited for the full moon ...

He stepped inside the chapel where he spotted the tourist dressed all in white who'd smiled at him earlier, at the water's edge. She was looking at the icons and, when she noticed him, she smiled at him again. Again he smiled back, then asked if she spoke English or French.

She was Dutch and knew both languages. A little Greek too, she added.

"I'm looking for the priest. Have you by any chance seen him?"

"No. He's probably still having a siesta. He knows better than anyone that the dead can wait, don't you think?"

With that joke she tried to start a conversation, but he excused himself and left the chapel to look for someone who could show him the priest's house. But the man had arrived and was talking to the young boy as if pleading with him to go home and let the dead girl rest in peace.

"They'd loved one another since primary school," he confided in English to Doctor Maras when he approached to explain why he had come to Leros.

The priest replied:

"I'm so sorry but I can't accept your wife's ashes for two reasons. We can't inter a Catholic in an Orthodox cemetery. Also, my church is opposed to cremation."

Doctor Maras walked out of the cemetery with heavy tread, the shadow of his body preceding him, growing longer and longer as if it were the ghost of his beloved searching the ground desperately for a place to rest. But no sooner had he gone twenty metres when he heard a voice behind him calling:

"Monsieur, monsieur!"

It was the Dutch woman, running toward him, gasping for breath.

"I heard you talking with the priest."

Yet another who was going to tell him how romantic and touching was his reason for coming here ...

"May I take the liberty of suggesting a place?"

She pointed to the mountain that overlooked the cemetery, the village, and Alinda Bay.

"There is nothing but rocks. You won't have to ask anyone's permission, no one will search for anything there, and I know where you can get a shovel."

He gazed at the mountain and his face lit up with a smile.

"Yes ..."

He looked for the sun in the sky.

"You won't have time today."

She was right. The sun was already sinking behind the mountain. If he were to go down and get the urn and the shovel and then come back up, this whole side would be in the dark.

"Since you'll be free this evening," the woman said, "would you give me the pleasure of dining with me? I know, you're in mourning but I can't stand to eat alone any more. Neither can you for that matter, I noticed earlier when I came back from my walk."

He wanted to spend this last evening alone with the ashes but how could he refuse when the Dutch woman had just relieved him of such a great concern? After all, dinner would last for an hour, two at most.

"You're right, I don't like eating alone in a restaurant."

"Nine o'clock then? At the café where I saw you at noon. It's the only one where they don't play that never-ending music and you can still hear the lapping of the waves."

28

SHE ARRIVED AT the café after a shower, hair done, scented, and wearing a dark silk dress with a generously plunging neckline that reminded Doctor Maras of the one that Alma had worn when they had their final meal together. As well, just like Alma over the past few years, before she sat down she would check the sources of light and choose a table where the lighting was softer, on the pretext that they would have a better view of the bay. On the other hand Alma, who usually applied perfume to all her pulse points, used none on Leros, the better to appreciate the scents all around her.

"One evening, during my first time on Leros," the Dutch woman said when she'd finished settling in at the table, "I was sitting here and, when I saw the full moon appear on the horizon, I wished for a power failure. Suddenly, I swear, all the lights went out. For a good half-hour, the moon alone lit up the island, as it must have done at the beginning of the world. At the age I was then, I saw it as a message from fate: Every day would be for me a blank page that I could cover as I wanted, according to my dreams and my wishes."

She heaved a sigh that raised her bosom and then, with the ease that people have when travelling, as if it were less painful to open up to a stranger one will never see again, she told him the story of her life.

Her name was Yannick Haakman. After studying Fine Arts in Amsterdam she had spent a year on Leros with her lover, he painting oils, she doing watercolours, until they knew every hue that earth, sky and sea can display between sunrise and sunset.

"Then we went back to Amsterdam where we did our best to tear one another to pieces."

She made a nervous little laugh that heaved her bosom again and her perfume wafted to him.

"I apologize. You came to dispose of your wife's ashes and I keep moaning and groaning. Were you married for a long time?"

"Twenty-four years."

"Twenty-four years! Bravo! What was her name? Was she a doctor too? Do you have any children?"

She was as curious as Alma and her questions kept taking him back to the past so that now and then he forgot where he was, despite the water lapping at his feet.

"An actress! How did you meet? You worked in such different fields."

Or:

"For some time now I've been seeing spots floating in my field of vision. What could that mean?"

Or else:

"Weren't you afraid when you were your daughter's age that you might make the wrong decision about your future? We're catapulted onto the stage of life without knowing our part, forced to improvise everything. And we aren't given a second chance to correct even one gesture, or to go over a word."

She listened to his replies with her head bent to one side, now and then watching the movement of his lips or his hands, then her gaze shifted to small boats swaying gently at the end of the jetty, then towards the lights of Agia Marina, the little harbour of Platanos that streamed across the bay to them, and a shadow of nostalgia swept over her face.

"Is there really an age when we aren't afraid of something? Even at my age and after all I've had by way of adventures, however much I wish, before I leave Leros for good, not for a power failure—those things only happen once in your life—I wish for an hour in the arms of a man, somewhere beside the water where there are no lights, but I don't dare ask for fear I'd be laughed at."

Doctor Maras looked down.

The woman's fingers fiddled briefly around her glass. Then:

"Yep, life doesn't have many parts for aging women only in the theatre and the movies."

She drained her glass in a gulp.

To avoid looking at her, he busied himself pouring what was left of the wine into the two glasses.

"Is that to give me courage?" she asked with the audacity of despair.

This time he did look her in the eye, gently.

"I want to spend the night with Alma."

The woman forced herself to smile.

"I'm happy for you. Your journey will end well and you'll go home with the satisfaction of your mission accomplished."

Raising her glass, she added:

"May your joie de vivre return very soon."

29

HE STAYED UP all night with the ashes and left his room before dawn when all the islanders were still in bed.

Leaving the lights of the hotel behind him he plunged into the silence and darkness of a winding road that rose between houses buried in eucalyptus and pines, climbed two hundred metres beyond the last one, hearing nothing but the crunch of pebbles under his feet.

When he finally stopped, the sky was beginning to turn pale at the approach of day, and wasps were already buzzing around a caper bush.

The air was mild and a pale halo surrounded the stars still twinkling in the sky, while below the hill, small crests fringed with foam broke over the feet of the sleeping village.

He put down the urn and began to dig the dew-damp soil while a few metres away from him two sparrows were quarrelling over the carcass of a cicada.

He did not waver until it was time to place the urn in the ground.

"I'll miss you, my love. Your laugh, your sparkling eyes, the energy you put into everything, that revived me when I came home in the evening, drained ... I was so happy with you that I thought I would never know the agony of loneliness. But don't worry: I'll let nothing show and I'll do my best to help Mélissa to find her way and to rediscover the beauty of the world. And one day I'll come back here with her children. I'll take them to see the place where I buried their grandmother's ashes and just as you'd have done I'll teach them to say jasmine, oregano, and thyme, not simply the words but how to recognize their scent ..."

In the distance, a rooster crowed. And as if it were Alma expressing her gratitude with that song, it was with a lighter heart that he took the shovel to cover the hole that now contained the ashes of his beloved, while the orange ball of the new day was emerging on the horizon, accompanied by the ringing of his cell phone.

He was so far away in his thoughts that for a moment, he was stunned.

"Hello?" he said finally.

"It's Franck. Sorry to wake you up but it's important."

"Did something happen?"

"Yes. Are you still on Leros?"

"Yes, why?"

"You mustn't leave the ashes there."

"Don't tell me you're going to bug me about that again?!"

"If you insist on respecting your wife's last wishes, listen to what I have to say."

"I'm listening."

"The letter Groslin had you read wasn't written by Alma. I've just found out. I'm shooting nights and the actress is a friend of Ninon Conti. We were chatting and she told me that this afternoon, Ninon talked to her about Alma's last wishes. I was right, eh? Groslin couldn't help boasting about it to his wife."

"Will you get to the point," Doctor Maras murmured. "What did Groslin tell his wife?"

"You won't breathe a word to Hélène? If she found out that you heard it from me she'd kill me. Promise?"

"I won't say a word. What did Groslin tell his wife?"

"Mélissa had contacted him to say you were coming to Paris and to tell him she'd send him a letter that she was going to write, imitating her mother's signature. That was why he made you wait another day. He wasn't in Marseille; he was waiting for the letter from your daughter."

There are people like that, embittered people who won't admit that others are not like them, and who try to contaminate them with their bitterness at all cost. And now that he had spat out his venom, Franck concluded dejectedly though in fact he was delighted:

"I knew this news would come as a crushing blow but I can't keep mum about a deceit like that, knowing how much you care about doing your very best at the task that Alma imposed on you."

30

LONG AFTER FRANCK had hung up he was still staring at his cell phone, lost, while the sun was giving back their colours to the sea and earth, and from the distance came the sound and its echo made by a woman beating a rug on her balcony.

When finally he emerged from his thoughts, he looked at his watch, realized that Mélissa hadn't gone to bed yet—in Montreal it was still the night before—and called her.

"When does your plane get in?" she asked blithely.

He wasn't the type to use cunning, especially not with his daughter with whom relations had always been candid. He asked her then straightforwardly if she had written the letter Groslin had given him.

"What? Who told you that? It can't be Groslin, you wouldn't have got to Leros."

So as not to involve Franck and screw things up in his marriage he told his daughter that he'd re-read the letter and decided that it wasn't Alma's writing. Too nervous and forced, as if someone were trying to imitate her.

"Too nervous?" Mélissa exclaimed. "She'd just found out that she was dying!"

"If she was so agitated, why hadn't she phoned Groslin instead of writing? Now that I think of it, why didn't Groslin bring me the envelope too?"

"Ask him."

"Mélissa, I can't take any more of this nightmare."

"What about me? I've just lost my mother, I don't know what's going on in my life, my father disappears just when I need him most, and all you can think of to tell me ... Shit! When will we see the end of those goddamn ashes?"

She could not go on; choked by a sob, she hung up.

When Doctor Maras came back to the hotel with the urn and the shovel, he was in such a state that when the Dutch woman, who was having breakfast in the garden, noticed him, she rushed over, saying:

"What happened? They wouldn't let you bury the ashes there either?"

He was so shaken he told her everything. But when he said that he was considering calling Serge Groslin, she burst out laughing, making her bosom heave.

"It seems as if you absolutely want to find out that she was happiest with another man!"

"Not at all. I just want to be sure ..."

"But it's obvious that your daughter wrote the letter. And it's very much to her credit. You ought to be wondering instead why she wrote it. It certainly wasn't to deceive you because her mother loved that French man, but to make you stop searching. And so that you would take care of her a little."

"She just had to ask me ..."

"And overwhelm you with her academic worries when you were mourning your wife?"

She wrapped an arm around him tenderly.

"Take the ashes home and try before it's too late to save what can still be saved. You don't know how lucky you are to have a daughter like her."

31

DOCTOR MARAS WAS back in Montreal twenty-six hours after departing Leros and one week after taking off for Paris. Mélissa hadn't come to the airport to meet him. He had called from Athens to let her know when he would arrive but her cell was still dead so he went home by taxi.

Mélissa had taken good care of her mother's garden. The lawn was mowed, the plants properly watered and growing green and vigorous. Even the bird-feeder was well-stocked with seeds. Mélissa wasn't there however to welcome her father. Doctor Maras took some time to unpack, shower, and make coffee to recharge his batteries: They would have lots to tell each other when his daughter came home.

He would say nothing more about the letter, he'd be careful not to preach to Mélissa about her education. Like him, she had opted for medicine when very young. While he had never regretted his choice, his daughter's enthusiasm had waned and she felt a need to make her way towards other horizons, devote her dreams to a profession not so "tedious." As if he'd become a surgeon just to make piles of money. But he won't stand up for himself, won't even try to convince her that talent, passion, and a vocation are not the prerogative of artists only. His daughter was living the first real heartbreak of her life. It was his duty to listen to her, to say the words that would most likely bring her strength and comfort in her suffering, to let her sail on her own. Even if she was toying with the idea of studying theatre like her mother, he wouldn't object, though he was well aware of the problems that she'd encounter along the way. It was he in fact who should change his attitude, look at his child through different eyes, with no illusions, and let her surprise him. Mélissa had both feet on the ground, she had curiosity and drive. She would just have to rediscover passion to start making progress again.

But there was no sign of Mélissa and two cups of coffee later he called Simon, her boyfriend, also a medical student.

"Is Mélissa at your place?"

"No."

"Do you know where she is?"

"I haven't spoken to her for a week."

"But I asked you to look after her while I was away. What happened?"

Simon hesitated to reply, as he had hesitated the previous Saturday.

"Was it because of school?"

"Did she talk to you about it?"

"I know she's not interested in medicine any more. Is that why you aren't speaking?"

"It's Mélissa who doesn't want to talk to me. She says she feels like she's at the bottom of a well and she intends to get out on her own."

Just like her father, who didn't talk about his problems until he had solved them, Alma would have said—Alma, the drama queen who at times seemed to get herself into difficult situations so she could talk afterwards and in detail about her woes and anxiety attacks.

"Thanks, Simon."

He hung up, thinking that his daughter was giving him the cold shoulder and had decided not to talk about her problems with her father either. And while he would rather have mortified his own flesh than see his child suffer, he would do as she wished and not call her friends to find her. Instead he should start to learn how to deal with the void that Alma had left. His lonely evenings had only begun.

32

HE WENT BACK to work on Monday, convinced that in a few days' time when Mélissa was not so angry with him, she would be back home. He couldn't imagine her doing anything else. But when a week went by without a word from her, he called her girlfriends. None of them knew where Mélissa was hiding. He called his sister-in-law too—perhaps Mélissa was hiding out in La Malbaie—but Carmen hadn't seen her niece since Alma's funeral. That is when he really started to worry, to imagine everything that a parent with no word from his child could imagine, and he leaped on the telephone every time it rang. His anxiety only faded when he was with a patient, then it came back with a vengeance when he found himself alone in the house. At dinner, it was as though he was eating soap. And when there was a reference on the news to the discovery of a young woman's body, he would shudder and the colour would drain from his face.

Carmen called every day to ask if he'd had any word about Mélissa. Though he was annoyed at his sister-in-law, as he was at all the people who had interfered with him in his search, he contained his anger and replied politely. Until his sister-in-law told him that she was coming to Montreal to help him in his investigations. He told her:

"You've done enough. I'll sort things out on my own."

He began by searching his daughter's room, but found nothing that could give him clues as to where she might have gone. Next, he called one of his patients, Detective Sergeant Dominic Ferro of the Montreal Police Force, to ask if Ferro could help him out.

"Has your daughter got a cell?" the policeman asked.

"Yes, but I've called and called and she never answers."

"Give me her number. At least I'll be able to locate her cell."

Two hours later, Detective Sergeant Ferro called to say that he had located the cell phone: in Saint-Hilaire. More precisely, in a property that now belongs to the Alliance universelle pour la Vie.

"And my brother-in-law didn't say a word," Doctor Maras said. "Probably to spite me, because I didn't leave the ashes to his sect."

"It's not a sect, Doctor. I looked it up. The Alliance universelle pour la Vie is a movement founded on justice and peace."

"Where all creatures are loved and respected for what they are."

"Those are honourable intentions, aren't they?"

"They're all vegetarians."

"Good for them."

"Sergeant, they're vegetarian because like his biblical namesake, their leader, Frère Isaïe, wants to make the lion eat straw with the ox."

"What are you getting at?"

"If he respects all creatures for what they are, why would he force the lion to eat straw?"

"Hmm. I hadn't thought of that."

Doctor Maras phoned Saint-Hilaire and asked for his daughter.

Zak picked up the phone. And told him:

"Mélissa's not ready to talk to you."

"When will she be ready?"

"Don't worry, she's fine. That's all I can say for the moment."

Far from reassuring him, his brother-in-law's words alarmed him even more, making his memory explode with everything he'd ever heard about certain sects in Quebec and the United States: swindling, confinement, torture and barbarism, even murder. Like the Alliance universelle pour la Vie, those sects were all led by slick sycophants with a capacity for sniffing out a person's weaknesses, for flattering his ego, for enhancing his self-image, hoodwinking and keeping under their thumbs with their hazy discourse men and women much older and more experienced than Mélissa. Once the fish had taken the hook, he was forbidden any contact with the outside world. Isolated and cloistered, some disciples had even let themselves be persuaded that their guru was the reincarnation of Christ. If he gave in to debauchery every night, it was solely to make him a "sinning Jesus" so that he could be an experienced magistrate when he would have to judge the sinners at the Last Judgment. Even more, one guru had convinced his disciples that there would be a tremendous cataclysm and that the only survivors would be those who would follow him into death. "True life happens afterwards," he would repeat to them. "And those who go with me will taste the greatest gift of all: immortality."

Not surprisingly, that night when his body finally let go, Doctor Maras fell into a sleep filled with harrowing dreams. He only remembered the last one, for he had to wake up to escape from it.

He is walking on a deserted beach. A skull lies on the sand. Is it Alma's? He wants to tell her about his anguish. But as soon as he touches the skull to lift it and talk to it, he finds himself in a large room, round and white like an igloo.

At the centre of the room, Silenus, the half-man and half-goat satyr, endowed with a huge paunch, hooves, and an erection the length of his forearm, is sprawled in a rocking chair.

"Was it you that brought me here?" Doctor Maras asks.

"Me?" Silenus says, bursting into loud drunken laughter—Wahahaha!—that shakes his erection like an enormous finger.

Doctor Maras looks for an exit but doesn't see a door or even a window.

He turns to the satyr again and, as if he doesn't notice the erection, tells him:

"Okay, it's my fault, it's all my fault. Now show me the door so that I can go and save my child."

The satyr grabs a remote, presses a button, and Doctor Maras is suddenly propelled into the air where he begins to fly in a circle, like a scale model of a remote-controlled airplane. Dizzy, he shouts to the satyr to turn off the remote and put him down but he is going so fast that his cries emerge from his mouth like a buzzing drone.

33

ANXIOUS AS HE was, he was unable to perform his work as ophthalmologist and surgeon with the necessary clear-headedness and composure. He cancelled all his appointments and spent the day at home, reading everything he'd found about Frère Isaïe on the Internet. Above all he wanted to know if any disciples had been able to leave the Alliance universelle pour la Vie and if so why, but he found nothing. He could have called Raymond Cholette, but the film director's intimacy with the sect made him suspect. So he called Paul Bienvenue, a journalist who had written a book about sects in Quebec. But he couldn't help him either. At most he repeated what Doctor Maras already dreaded: To better manipulate a young recruit, a guru would control her every thought, every dream, every moment of her life, and the longer he held sway over the recruit, the harder it would be for her to free herself. And so he must act quickly: Vulnerable as Mélissa was just then, it would not take long before she submitted both body and soul to the authority of Frère Isaïe. But how could he persuade her to leave that imposter? She wouldn't even speak to him.

The more Doctor Maras pondered the situation, the more the house was transformed into a vast, creepy dwelling surrounded by a garden that gave him a pang every time he looked at it, for it represented the overwhelming evidence of his guilt. If anything happened to his daughter, even if he moved, the memory of that garden would flay him until he died, obscuring everything else he had done, and leave him with a single image of himself, that of a father who had contributed to the doom of his daughter. And Paul Bienvenue added to his distress when he called back at the end of the day to say:

"I remembered something that happened three years ago, at the estate of the Alliance universelle pour la Vie in Saint-Hilaire. The death of a young disciple called Stéphanie Filion."

"Why didn't Detective Sergeant Ferro say anything about it?"

"Maybe to keep you from worrying. Actually, the police had concluded it was an accident. I didn't refer to it in my book either or I'd have been prosecuted for libel."

"What happened to Stéphanie Filion?"

"At Saint-Hilaire, every resident is responsible for a daily task: cooking, the vegetable garden, laundry … Stéphanie Filion did the housekeeping. According to witnesses her hands were wet when she picked up a worn electrical wire …"

"And you don't believe that version?"

"According to Stéphanie Filion's mother, her daughter

called her the night before to tell her she was pregnant by Frère Isaïe. She wanted her mother to make her an appointment for an abortion. She couldn't do it herself; Frère Isaïe watched her like a hawk. Not only did he think abortion was murder, he wanted Stéphanie to keep the child and persuade the other members of the sect that he'd been conceived by theogamy and was the new Messiah."

"Why didn't she go along?"

"She'd stopped believing in her guru. Again, according to her mother. One night while he was sleeping, Stéphanie had discovered piles of comic books under his bed. Leafing through them, she'd realized that it was from them that he lifted his grand statements and his ideas. She had also discovered that he suffered from chronic constipation."

"A vegetarian?"

"Precisely."

"And the police did nothing?"

"You can't arrest someone for eating meat and reading comics on the sly. Moreover, police forensics had confirmed his version of the accident. And Stéphanie's mother was heavily into the booze and she tended to ramble. In fact it was her alcoholism that had driven her daughter to look for another family. Feeling rejected, the mother could have made it all up to take revenge on the parent whom her daughter had preferred to her."

"What do *you* think?"

"I spent enough time studying sects to know that morality and cover-ups always go hand in hand. But the law can't do anything unless there has been a punishable offence or if a complaint has been lodged. And you can't lodge a complaint. Your daughter is an adult in the eyes of the law and she went to Saint-Hilaire of her own free will."

34

DID YOU KNOW, Alma, where you were the happiest? Probably not or you'd have named the place. And because you couldn't decide where you were the happiest you wanted your husband to decide for you. Look what that led to. Not only has he lost his wife, because you hadn't consulted your doctor as he had asked you, your dithering about where you'd been the happiest may now rob him of what is dearest in the world to him.

"That's all I need!" the poor man cries out. "For that son-of-a-bitch to add to my woes by honouring my daughter with his blessèd seed! If I want to see my child again, I'll have to concede that the fruit of her womb is the new Messiah! Even worse, if Mélissa refuses to give in to that megalomaniac's demands, cruel and vindictive as he must be, she'll end up like Stéphanie Filion. Ah, why did I bring her to Saint-Hilaire? Why didn't I just bury the ashes in our garden?"

He wants to call Carmen and Pauline and all the others and tell them that if they hadn't misled him with their asinine suggestions, he wouldn't have gone to Paris.

Then he tells himself: "You could've ignored them, you moron. So don't add to the mess you've made of things. Instead of lighting into the others, find a way to warn your daughter of the danger she's in; save her while there's still time."

But search though he may, poor man, as soon as an idea comes to mind, he refutes it, sweeping it aside either because it would only lead to his arrest or because it would alienate his daughter even more, until she would accede willingly to the desires of her spiritual father, just to spite the biological one. And as if he weren't suffering enough from being surrounded by the vestiges of his life as father and husband, now there is a new convoy of images in his mind, with Frère Isaïe murmuring his esoteric crap while driving his sanctimonious cock into his beloved daughter. His helplessness is so profound and his mood so dark that tears come to his eyes.

Can you see them, Alma, can you see his tears? If there is anything you can do to stop them, don't you think that now is the time? Otherwise it would vindicate Nicole Gouin who still thinks that your last wishes were only meant to piss off the living so that they would go on talking about you long after your passing. I'm sure you had a few scores to settle with some people, but with your own husband? "He's the most upstanding, the most considerate man in the world," you would tell your friends. "When I give up hope about people I just have to think about him and I am reconciled with humanity." What has happened since then? Were you angry with him because he had a strong heart, as Franck maintains, and would be staying alive to enjoy it? Even if it were true, do you have to imitate Medea and destroy your child too in order to make your husband pay for it? "My Alma was funny and witty, even though she preferred to perform tragedy," he says about you still. "She had a big heart as well. Sick perhaps but big to the end." Could he have been wrong about that too?

35

"PAPA, WHERE DO tears come from?"

She was ten years old. She no longer toddled along behind him, asking question after question, but sat across from him to talk and listen to his answers, face taut with concentration.

"Tears come from the tear glands, which are under the bones, there, above each eye. They travel along small ducts and bathe the eyes to keep them moist and protect them from infections, then they seep towards the inside corner of the eyes and from there into the nose. When there are too many tears because a person is angry or sad, they run down onto the cheeks."

"Why are they salty?"

She'd forgotten the explanation he had given her on Leros a few summers before.

"Tears are salty because they come from the circulation of your blood. And our blood contains salt because long, long ago our ancestors came from the sea. When you cry because you're sad, the composition of your tears changes but we don't yet know why."

"When I grow up I'm going to be a doctor like you and I'll find out why."

She adored TV series about medical teams and, while her friends envied her having a mother who was an actress, after she saw the production of *Romeo and Juliet* in which Alma played Lady Capulet, Mélissa only commented on the scene in which Juliet swallows a potion that will make her appear to be dead.

"Is there really a potion like that? Does the heart stop beating? No? So if Romeo had put his ear against her chest he'd have heard her heartbeats? Why didn't he? He was always talking about his heart when he saw her, why didn't he think about it? Good thing they didn't have children. Romeo might talk like an angel but you couldn't really count on him in an emergency as we could count on papa."

Doctor Maras sank into the deepest despair when the memory of that scene made the embryonic thought form in his head. He turned it over and over, studied it from every angle, and when he was finally convinced that it could serve his objectives, he thanked his wife for having put her pride aside that one time and accepted a supporting role. Then he blew his nose vigorously to get rid of the tears still there and, having got his voice back, and his composure, he called Saint-Hilaire and this time asked for Zak.

He told him:

"Does your offer still hold?"

"Change your mind again? How come?" his brother-in-law demanded, voice full of mistrust.

"Mélissa convinced me that her mother was happiest in her garden."

"You have a garden."

"The house is too big for me now that Mélissa is gone so I'm going to sell it."

Zak could understand that but he remained on guard.

"I'll come by tomorrow for the ashes."

"I want to put them into Mélissa's hands directly."

"She is not ready to go out yet."

"I'll bring them to Saint-Hilaire, with her things. Will she be there tomorrow?"

"Yes."

Doctor Maras smiled. A few hours earlier the world had turned into a purgatory, where he had nothing left to lose but his remorse and pain. Now he felt that the world was being renewed, its light returning. He called Simon, his daughter's boyfriend, to tell him that Mélissa was at the oasis of the Alliance universelle pour la Vie, in Saint-Hilaire, and that he would need his help to get her out.

He also called 911 to reserve an ambulance. Called his secretary too and asked her to bring him a flask of atropine, the alkaloid extracted from belladonna. Next, he piled logs in the fireplace and lit a fire. In the middle of the summer. And while the logs burned up and produced the ashes that he needed, he went from one window to another and opened them wide so that the scents and sounds of life would enter and fill his house once again.

36

HOW HE HAS been waiting for this moment! How impatiently does he head for Saint-Hilaire the next day! And when finally he walks into Zak's place weighed down by the urn and with Simon lugging a big cardboard box, what a burst of love and tenderness does he feel rising in him when he sees his child again!

There aren't so many people in the house this time and the greeting is not so warm, as if they suspect him of coming back, and with his daughter's boyfriend in tow, only to persuade her to return with them. And when he approaches Mélissa, Frère Isaïe approaches as well to hear what he is going to say. But Doctor Maras merely asks his daughter how she is.

"I'm fine," she snaps, without embracing him.

He goes on smiling all the same, quickly dispelling the anxiety of the blowhard who's keeping an eye on him and that of his flock who suspiciously are checking out Simon and the second box that he's taking out of the car. Doctor Maras asks for silence and then, calling on everything he learned from Alma when he gave her cues, he says with a very serious look on his face, but without a frown and with his emotions under control:

"My wife, God rest her soul, asked me to leave her ashes in the place where she had been the happiest. I wanted to bury them in our garden. Zak told me that was the wrong garden. Others said it was the wrong city, the wrong country even. By inclination or because I've been conditioned by my profession, I could not do things by halves. I had to check out every hypothesis before I made any decision. And so I ended up at the outermost reaches of the Mediterranean. If I brought the ashes back to Quebec it's because I concluded that what made Alma happiest was her child. And as that child has decided to move in with you I would like to leave her mama's ashes here. Your garden isn't my wife's any more but it's still an oasis of love, virtue, and harmony, and as Alma did for thirty years as a thespian, the inhabitants of this oasis are working to ennoble people's minds."

The inhabitants in question are so flattered, moved, and reassured that it might well have ended with hugs and kisses all around. Mélissa alone seems more surprised than convinced by her father's spiel. She has always known him as a man who says what he thinks, in few words, clear and precise, and here he is smooth-talking his hosts because he certainly hasn't changed his mind about the oasis any more than a cat would about water, or seen God, whom she hears him mention for the first time in her life, on the road to Leros. But why is he doing all this? she wonders, looking him over to plumb the depths of his thinking while her papa, turning to her now, says:

"Mélissa, since you have listened to your heart and your heart has told you to settle here, I've brought your clothes in these boxes and in this urn, your mama's ashes. Not only will they stay with her beloved daughter, my wife will have a magnificent monument that will prolong her existence by showing to posterity the place where she is buried."

No, he has never spewed out so much baloney, even as a teenager trying to impress a girl. But the life of his child is at stake and he is ready to do and say anything to gain the trust of her jailer and free her from his influence. And to achieve his ends, after giving the urn to Mélissa, he allows himself one last blast of hot air because as a physician, he knows that it's all a matter of dosage and that if the dose is wrong, a tranquillizer can become a poison.

"Since your heart also tells you, my child, to pursue your education here," he says, "I will pay to the Alliance universelle pour la Vie the hundred thousand dollars that your mother and I had set aside for your schooling."

"Oh!" say the others, as if they've seen an angel fly by.

"Brothers, sisters," says Isaïe, the great mystifier, now himself totally mystified. "Our greatest joy is to see an ever-growing portion of humanity rallying to our cause. Today that joy is all the greater because along with the ashes of our dear sister Alma we are welcoming among us a man of a type that is increasingly rare in this world corrupted by lies, selfishness, and deceit, a principled man who is highly intelligent too, and generous to boot. May he whose name is the flower which attracts the bees that have gone astray achieve all his desires, the very summit of prosperity, and prolong the number of his years in perfect health."

"Amen!" the others agree.

Mélissa still says nothing.

Ah, children. Doctor Maras knew that they are much less lenient than a parent is with them but still he'd hoped that his daughter would react, if not to the boxes of clothes then at least to the promised donation of a hundred thousand dollars to the Alliance universelle pour la Vie. But Mélissa is blinded by her resentment and her pride, unaware of the heavy toll they could demand of her. Her father who is well aware of that decides then to go into action. He rubs his chest, grimacing, as if he were having heartburn, then asks Simon to bring him a glass of water.

Simon brings him a glass of water.

Once he has drunk the water, Doctor Maras smiles again and says:

"Come into the garden, my friends, let us pray that our beloved Alma, whom the Eternal has received in the splendour and bliss of heaven, shows us the earthly spot where she would like the monument to her memory to be erected."

37

IN THE GARDEN they form a circle, they link hands, and intone a litany in which, after every line sung by the women, the men, ecstatic, respond with the same refrain.

Creator of beings, of water and earth.
In heaven, in heaven soon we shall meet!
Guide thy daughter Alma towards our circle.
In heaven, in heaven, soon we shall meet!
For her ashes we seek rest eternal.
In heaven, in heaven, soon we shall meet!

A refrain that makes Doctor Maras shiver despite the blazing mid-July sun. Unless the shivers are caused by the atropine of which, as they had agreed, Simon had added a few drops to his glass of water. Only a few drops, of course, to slow down his heart rate, not speed it up, and to knock him out. Ever since Doctor Maras drained the glass, Simon has not taken his eyes off him and when he sees him falter he hurries to support him, crying out:

"Something wrong, Doctor?"

Mélissa spins around and, when she sees her father's face turn red and only the whites of his eyes, her features come alive at last and she cries out:

"Papa! What's the matter?"

Ah! The sound of that "papa." Rain in the desert. And he smiles, in spite of the sudden nausea that strikes him, he smiles and while the singers, cut off in their mystical delirium, look on, absorbed and silent, he replies, dry-mouthed:

"It's probably the heat, the emotion ..."

Mélissa lays her hand on her father's forehead, then on his pulse, but he is already collapsing in Simon's arms—the young man has been standing behind him to break his fall. His eyes flutter briefly and, when they close abruptly, the crowd lets out a cry, two women nearly faint, and Frère Isaïe shrieks at Zak and his wife:

"Don't stand there! Call an ambulance!"

He wants Doctor Maras to stay alive, at least until he has signed the hundred-thousand dollar cheque he promised. But Simon has already taken out his cell and punched in a number. And when the ambulance he calls finally arrives, Frère Isaïe grabs the urn and tells Liza to stow it somewhere safe. He would like to hold Mélissa hostage too, to make sure that her father will come back with the cheque, but when he suggests to her that it might be best if Zak were to go with her father in the ambulance, she dismisses him with a wave of her hand. In any event, the paramedics have already been ordered to let no one but the young woman come onboard. As Simon was supposed to drive Doctor Maras' car back, they had also been ordered to administer an antidote—physostigmine or pilocarpine—in case of a paralysis of the respiratory tract.

All that's left for Frère Isaïe to do is pray for Doctor Maras' speedy recovery, and the others chime in, under the fake palm trees while the ambulance drives away at breakneck speed with siren howling, and Mélissa in the back at her father's side.

"What got into you?" Alma asks her husband. "Taking that poison! It's insane!"

A brief digression: ingestion of atropine also produces hallucinations. And in his delirium Doctor Maras sees himself at his fireplace, cleaning up whatever ashes are left from the logs, making little mounds of them, then stuffing these last traces of his nightmare into a garbage bag while Alma is reprimanding him rather than congratulating him for having taken away their child from the oasis at Saint-Hilaire.

"What if Simon gave you the wrong dose? And if your heart had given up? Did you think of that?"

"You're the one who gave me the idea."

"*After all the years and love I've given you and all your oaths to me*, you dump my ashes under a stupid plastic palm tree to rush back to Leros to gawk in the moonlight at your Dutch matron's boobs, and you have the nerve to say it was my idea? *Rotten! Heart-rotten! That is the only word for you!*"

"You're jealous."

"Me?"

"When you start quoting the characters you played ..."

"Don't make me laugh. Jealous. Me. Of an overweight, middle-aged biddy."

"You are jealous! Because I'm the man of your life? The one you were happiest with?"

"Spare me your male chauvinist ideas. All they do is prick my anger not my jealousy. Especially when I think about our beautiful garden. My Mélissa took such good care of it. Still you dumped my ashes in Saint-Hilaire, so they wouldn't trouble your conscience when your rubenesque playmate comes here."

"Alma, my love, that urn didn't contain your ashes."

"Oh Lord!"

"Now what?"

"When Mélissa finds out that it was just for show ..."

"I would rather face her anger than her silence."

"And what if she goes back to those idiots to take revenge for that mystification?"

"I'm going to reason with her, tell her about Stéphanie Filion. After that, if she still wants to go though with the Immaculate Conception con ..."

"My house will be all yours and your whore's. Ah! You should have left me at Père-Lachaise."

"DON'T START THAT AGAIN!"

"You don't have to shout ..."

"I HAVE GOOD REASON!"

"You're right. Relax. Mélissa needs you. We'll make peace and I'll let you sleep, okay?"

And so it goes. We always end up going to sleep. And so they did, each in his own world.

ABOUT THE AUTHOR

PAN BOUYOUCAS is a Montreal prize-winning writer, playwright, and translator whose novels and plays have been translated into several languages. Two of his novels were written originally in English: *The Man Who Wanted to Drink Up the Sea*, which was selected by France's FNAC as one of the 12 best novels of 2005, and *The Tattoo*, which was longlisted for the 2012 Re-Lit Award.

ABOUT THE TRANSLATOR

SHEILA FISCHMAN is the award-winning translator of nearly 200 works of fiction from Quebec. She has been awarded the Molson Prize in the Arts and is a Member of the Order of Canada and a chevalier of the Ordre national du Québec. She lives in Montreal.

Printed in April 2018
by Gauvin Press,
Gatineau, Québec